VIEW FROM A BLIND BRIDGE

VIEW FROM A BLIND BRIDGE

JUNE CONSIDINE

POOLBEG

First published in 1992 by
Poolbeg Press Ltd
Knocksedan House,
Swords, Co Dublin, Ireland

© June Considine 1992

The moral right of the author has been asserted.

A catalogue record for this book is available from The British Library.

ISBN 1 85371 244 2

Cover design by Judith O'Dwyer
Set by Mac Book Limited in ITC Stone 10/14
Printed by The Guernsey Press Company Ltd,
Vale, Guernsey, Channel Islands

To Jim Kilroy—whose deep love of horses was the inspiration for this story.
Also to the memory of Sophie the donkey, whose gentle life was ended so cruelly.

Contents

1

The News Breaks

"We're moving to Stonyford," said Mrs Hackett, and sat back to watch the reaction of her family.

Her eldest son, Ben, shot his fist into the air in a victory salute. Cindy, her eldest daughter, asked if Susie Moone was also moving and, when assured that she was, went back to watching television. The twins, Dave and Steve, wondered if they would still be able to buy the *Beano* and *Dandy* each week. Mrs Hackett said that Stonyford was a village in Dublin, not a planet in outer space, and she was sure it would be full of well-stocked newsagents selling comics. Jean, her youngest child, said nothing at all. She climbed on to her father's knees and rubbed his face, trying to ease away the lines of disappointment.

"Gob-smacked—that's what I am," muttered Mr Hackett.

Since he heard that Wheatfield Flats were to be demolished, he had hoped that his family would be rehoused in one of the town houses that were being built by Dublin Corporation in the centre of Dublin. But the months of waiting and wondering were over. The decision had been made and the Hackett family was on the move.

"Would someone mind telling me where this Stonyford place is supposed to be?" asked Mr Hackett, in much the same tone as he would enquire the whereabouts of an execution chamber.

"Look, there it is." Ben was thirteen years old, tall and fair-skinned, with a thatch of straw-blond hair falling over his forehead. He spread a map of Dublin across the table and moved his finger in a north-western direction, to a small village that had remained untouched by progress until one morning when the villagers had woken to the throb of bulldozers and an army of builders moving across the green fields. Within a short time rows of grey, two-storey houses stretched along the bank of Four-Mile River. The building of River View had begun. The last phase of development was almost finished and Ben, after living all his life in a high-rise block of flats, would soon be transported to a cul-de-sac shaped like a horseshoe and called River View Avenue.

But Mr Hackett had no time for maps, only memories. A sentimental man by nature, he told his family that it would break his heart to leave this snug little community. How could he live without the shrill cries of street traders and the comforting throb of traffic?

"Will you stop talking rubbish or I'll blow you into the middle of next week," threatened his wife. "One extra sardine wouldn't be able to draw breath in this place." Five children had been reared in the two-bedroomed flat, so she brushed aside her husband's complaints with the same energy she used to swat a troublesome fly. "This flat should have been pulled down long before Noah's Ark ever set sail. Just imagine it, Ben. A new house. And a garden to the front and the back of us."

"Can I bring Brandy with me?" asked Ben, hopefully.

Brandy was a dog that Ben had found along the bank of the Grand Canal, lying injured after he had been hit by a car. Ben carried him home and placed his injured leg in a splint. Within a week of his recovery, Brandy had chewed the edge of the table cloth, ripped the legs of Ben's new jeans and eaten the roast chicken which Mrs Hackett had left to settle on the kitchen table.

"Either that thing goes or I'm packing up and bailing out," declared Mrs Hackett in a voice that brooked no argument.

Ben had persuaded Mr Barrett, the janitor of Wheatfield Flats, to look after Brandy and Old Barro (as he was nicknamed by the tenants) agreed, claiming one half of the dog for himself and allowing Ben to own the other half.

At the mention of the dog's name, Mrs Hackett's mood changed. "If you think for one minute that I'm going to mess up my new house with that thing you can think again!" She shook her finger sternly at her son. "You can have a goldfish if you like."

Ben treated this concession with the contempt it deserved.

"And you needn't bother looking at me like that," she ordered. "I've had it up to here with your pigeons and snails and mice and whatever else takes your fancy. As for that frog spawn stuff, I've been flushing it down the toilet so often that the sewers of Dublin must be crawling with frogs!"

"Not to mention Sheba," prompted Cindy, grinning at her brother.

Mrs Hackett shuddered at the memory of the tiny

rodent that Ben had introduced to his family when he was six years old. She had suffered a violent attack of hysterics on discovering that the furry creature with the unblinking eyes, nestling under her son's jumper and sharing her son's food, was not a hamster, as Ben had insisted, but a rat he had discovered in the basement of the flats when it was only a baby.

From his youngest days, Ben had been conscious of certain feelings that he experienced when he was close to animals, a shivery sense of warmth flowing through his body. In the same instant strange-sounding words would come into his head. He had no trouble pronouncing those words and the animals seemed to understand what he was saying to them. Sometimes he could communicate with them, understand their feelings, just by touching them. He accepted this sensation as something that set him apart from other boys but did not think very much about it. "Daft loving," was his mother's name for it, and Ben was content enough with that.

That evening, he called for his friend Danny Moone, who lived in the flat above the Hacketts. Danny was small, dark and wiry, the wild boy, full of tensed-up energy and mischief. He loved people and noise and excitement. He roamed the city streets with the older boys from the flats, played his mouth-organ in Grafton Street on a Saturday afternoon and stood in shop doorways, filling his head with loud rock music.

Ben had no interest in rock music or crowded city streets and his dream was to live in the country. The fact that the two boys were so different had never interfered with their friendship, and with Ben, the quiet one, the dreamer, Danny relaxed, and their friendship flowed along as easily as sea overlapping sand.

Ben lifted his hand to knock on Danny's front door, hesitating when he heard the raised voices of Mr and Mrs Moone. The sounds of their anger carried easily through the thin walls. Sometimes when Ben was in Danny's flat, he could hear Mr and Mrs Moone arguing in another room. Danny would keep talking, laughing, cracking jokes non-stop, pretending that the raised voices of his parents were just the background sounds from a television programme. But Ben knew that Danny never wanted him around when his parents argued.

As he turned to leave, the door opened and his friend appeared. Danny's eyes looked gritty and red-rimmed, as if he had rubbed them too hard. He stood still when he saw Ben and scowled. "What do you want?"

"Are you coming out? I'm bringing Brandy to the canal," Ben replied, ignoring the abrupt tone just as he ignored the raised voices behind the door.

Danny shrugged and slammed the door. He slouched his shoulders and shoved his hands into the pockets of his jeans. They collected Brandy from Old Barro. The dog ran along the bank of the canal with a paint-tin lid in his mouth. Danny followed, kicking an empty Seven-Up can and complaining bitterly. Many of the tenants from Wheatfield would be rehoused in newly built houses in the centre of their old community. But some, like the Moones and Hacketts, would be moving away from the city and settling in Stonyford.

"It's out in the sticks. Culchie land," Danny snorted when Ben talked about the rivers they could swim and the hills they could climb. "No one's going to pack me off to the backside of nowhere."

Ben flung the lid into the canal and Brandy, panting with excitement, dived in after it. No matter how fast or how far the paint-tin lid dropped, Brandy's razor-sharp eyes would spot it and he would clench it in his teeth before it reached the bottom.

Danny's face was expressionless as he watched the dog. "He says he's going to leave," he muttered. "He says he can't take the pressure any more."

"Don't mind your father. He's only saying that." Ben flung the lid into the water once more. "He'd never leave you and Susie."

"I think he will, especially if they knock down the flats. He says that if anyone tries to tell him where he's going to live, he'll soon tell them where to get off!"

Every summer, Danny climbed Bray Head with his father. They fished together on the banks of the canal, and whenever Ireland played an international soccer match at Lansdowne Road, Danny's father brought him along. They wrapped the green scarves around their necks, cheering and singing from the terraces until they were hoarse. But when his father drank too much, he lost his temper at the slightest provocation and his voice, shouting at Danny, could be heard all over the flats. "Get out of the way, stupid, or I'll fist you into the middle of next week."

On such occasions, Danny would call for Ben, doing his comedian routine for the Hackett family, reducing the younger members to shrieks of laughter. But eventually he would stop talking and his lips would press together in a thin line, as if his teeth had locked together.

This was not the first time that Mr Moone had threatened to leave his family. But it was the first time

Ben heard the fear in his friend's voice that it might happen.

Brandy ran between Danny's legs and almost toppled him into the canal. "Stupid mutt! Will you watch where you're going!" he yelled, kicking out at the dog, who nipped nimbly out of reach. "Next time I throw that lid in, I'm going to load it with a cement block." His voice had returned to normal. "Not that I care what he does. If he wants to go, let him! I'm sick listening to the pair of them, going on at each other all the time. It makes me sick, so it does." He turned abruptly, walking so fast in front of Ben that his shape was soon hidden by the November mist that had descended over the banks of the canal.

A week later the two boys decided to visit Stonyford. Danny looked cold in his short denim jacket. His face had a pinched expression when he stared at Ben, sensing his friend's excitement, which was in sharp contrast to his own feelings.

Mappo Deane went with them. He also lived in Wheatfield and was a thin, lanky boy who wore his black hair shaved at the back with the long top layers drawn into a ponytail. His real name was Matthew. But Ben could never remember calling him anything but Mappo. Mappo claimed to have been born with a map of the world imprinted on his brain. His friends believed that this was an exaggeration. It was only a map of Dublin.

His spare time was spent at either Dun Laoghaire Harbour or Heuston Station where trains arrived from the south and west of Ireland. He called himself the world's only "travel busker" and stood beneath a painted sign that read, "Lost? Confused? Consult the Human

Map." In his hand he carried a pad and pencil. In his head he carried a detailed knowledge of the city, every street, monument, historic building, hotel, car park and shop. Visitors to the city, intrigued by the sight of the young busker with the friendly grin, stopped to ask him directions and dropped money into the plastic box at his feet. He drew maps for them, detailing the routes they should take and any other information that would be useful to them. Mappo was as much a part of Dublin city as the pigeons that strutted beside the wheels of passing cars. He hated the idea of moving, and demanded to know how he could earn his living in Stonyford when no one in their right minds would want to visit the kip in the first place.

When they reached Stonyford, Ben saw the grassy spread of land known as Clemartin's Stretch and Four-Mile River running like a silver thread along its bank. River View Estate was a sweeping sprawl of houses on the opposite bank. Danny said it was "the pits" and that Clemartin's Stretch would soon be cemented over and built upon in the same way. On the way home in the bus, Mappo switched on his Walkman radio so that he would not have to listen to the two friends, who had a bitter argument over whether or not the move to Stonyford was a good thing.

By January, Mr Moone had carried out his threat and left his family.

"He just walked away from them without as much as a word," said Mrs Hackett. "They say he's gone off with some young one and she's going to have his baby. I'd say that's the last his family will see of him for a while."

"Good riddance, that's what I say," said Mr Hackett.

"He was never any good to them."

"But the boy loves him," replied Mrs Hackett. "It's going to have a bad effect on him, mark my words. You should call up and see him, Ben. I hardly ever see the two of you together any more." She made numerous pots of tea for Danny's mother, who wept in the Hacketts' kitchen for a week. Then Mrs Moone dried her eyes and got on with the business of living. Danny told Ben that his father's departure didn't bother him in the least. "I hate him!" he said in a cold voice and refused to discuss the subject any further.

But his face filled with resentment as the March date for departure drew nearer.

For a week before the people of Wheatfield left, they held farewell parties with the adults singing "The Rare Auld Times" over and over again. Even Danny laughed when Mrs Sheridan formed a chain and they danced the conga up and down the stairs and all along the corridors of the flats. Ben was kissed three times by Danny's sister, Susie Moone.

"Just in case we never meet again, Ben," she sighed tragically and the two of them laughed because they were going to live next door to each other in Stonyford.

"I'm moone-struck," gasped Ben and Susie kissed him one more time for luck.

When the removal van came to load up the Hacketts' furniture, Ben stood in the centre of the cement garden and gazed around the desolate flats with their silent balconies. How quickly Wheatfield had lost its quirky spirit once the people left. There was a sprinkling of cherry blossom on the trees in their squares of clay. But the blossoms wilted as if they knew this would be their last season of bloom. When Ben brought Brandy to the canal for his farewell walk, the dog stood at the edge of the bank and watched the paint-tin lid float down among the reeds and out of sight. Then he gave a faint whimper and licked the boy's hand. Ben could read the message in his eyes: you're leaving me and I don't want to play this game with anyone else.

He could hear the dog whining when he left him back with Old Barro.

In the basement of the flats, where the musty smell of buried secrets had once thrilled and terrified him, Ben cried, quietly and secretly, until his mother's voice called him back to the family. The removal van was ready to leave.

2

Exploring Charney House

From the beginning, Danny was determined not to settle into his new home. "My father'd have come back to Wheatfield. But he'll never come to live in this kip," he told Ben. When weeks passed into months and he heard no word from his father, it gave him one more reason to hate Stonyford. Although the Moones and the Hacketts lived next door, the two boys seldom called for each other.

Ben began to spend less time in River View. Away from the concrete and the hum of cement-mixers, there were country lanes and the magnificent wilderness of Cypress Hill to be explored. Charney House was a large, tumbledown house that had once belonged to a family of the same name. It stood on the summit of Cypress Hill and Ben discovered the old ruin soon after moving to River View. Danny went with him once but he had no interest in climbing the crumbling walls or exploring the overgrown gardens surrounding it. He preferred to hang out on the stretches of land that ran like green ribbons through River View and were nicknamed "the wastelands" by the teenagers. In a section of the wastelands that sloped down towards Four-Mile River, a cider gang gathered at night, older boys, who built bonfires in the grassy hollows and drank from green plastic flagons.

In September, Ben heard that the old house was due to be demolished and returned there for a final visit. He tried to persuade Danny to come with him but his friend was not interested in "stupid kids' games."

To reach Stonyford Village, which was a mile from River View, Ben had to cross a hump-backed bridge, known locally as the blind bridge. It twisted sharply in the centre and the hump was so high that it was impossible for those driving across to see if traffic was coming from the other end. Traffic lights had been installed and the cars at one end of the bridge moved only when the cars at the opposite end had been signalled to stop.

Cypress Hill rose beyond the village, dipping into valleys of gorse and heather and wild rocky ledges. It was criss-crossed with shady lanes where the wealthy population of Stonyford lived. They had been bitterly opposed to the building of River View, even though they were separated from the estate by the village and Four-Mile River. Their homes were surrounded by high hedges and protected by electronic gates.

Ben could see riding paddocks and flat-roofed stables in the grounds of the big houses. Ponies poked their heads over hedges and their nostrils quivered with excitement when he spoke to them and breathed into their faces. When he reached Charney House, a "No Trespassing" notice hung on the gatepost. He ignored it and climbed the high gate.

Wooden boards had been nailed across the windows but he found a small back window that had not been boarded up. His face was flushed when he finally wriggled into the room. Rain had stripped the wallpaper from the walls and encouraged scraggy weeds to push through the floorboards. In the dim light he saw a small figure in white, standing perfectly still, watching him. The white robe seemed to shimmer in the dim light, to part into two separate pieces as the ghostly figure began to move towards him. He tried not to scream and stood still, petrified with fear.

"Hey Bug-eyes! What are you staring at?" The voice rudely interrupted his trance.

"Not much," he replied, feeling his heartbeat returning to normal when the phantom turned into a plump girl who looked about twelve years old. She was wearing a pair of white, baggy jeans and a white T-shirt. Her black hair was long and straight, with a parting on one side. When she pushed it back from her forehead, he noticed that her hand trembled. But she was cool, staring at him as if he had no right to intrude on her space. "Who told you you could come in here?" she asked in an accusing tone.

"I'm very sorry," Ben snapped. "I didn't realise I had to get written permission."

"You don't need written permission. But there is a notice outside that says 'No Trespassing!'"

"I didn't see you paying any attention to it!"

"Maybe I don't have to." She began to laugh. "You should have seen your face when you came through that window. You thought I was a ghost."

"Don't kid yourself. I didn't think that! Not for one minute."

"Liar."

"Even if I did, you wouldn't be the first ghost I've seen

around this place." Ben lowered his voice and glanced around.

"Oh, fade out!" she drawled. "I suppose you're going to tell me that this dump is haunted."

"I don't have to tell you. Look around you. They're everywhere, the spirits of the damned." He pitched his tone even lower. "I'll show you where they rest. That's if you have the nerve to look."

"Lead the way!" she ordered briskly, following him from the room.

Twilight cast long shadows on the walls and the wind whistled an eerie tune through the empty rooms. Shapes moved before them like cobwebby claws. Doors creaked. It was easy to imagine the ghosts of the Charney family groaning in anguish under the rotting floorboards. But his companion stayed calm, even when cobwebs brushed her face and rustling sounds suggested that bats had been disturbed by the sound of their voices.

Then she told him a story of Desmond Charney, heir to the family fortune, who had been buried alive within the walls of Charney House by his jealous younger brother. Every night, on the stroke of midnight, this gruesome skeleton reached out with a bony hand and gripped the hair of whoever was unfortunate enough to be walking past. It was a deadly grip that never eased. Dead bodies had been found, rooted to the spot, with bald patches on their heads. She stared, straight-faced, at him. "Honest. I swear it's true."

He scoffed, snorted with laughter and felt goose-pimples on his scalp, loving and hating the horror she was creating around them. When they finally climbed back out through the little window, her T-shirt had ripped and was covered in dust. They walked across the bed of a dried-out lake. Ben tried to imagine what it would look like with swans swimming on it and fish darting through a deep-green forest of water-reeds. They stopped when they reached the biggest horse-chestnut tree. "If you climb this tree, you'll be able to see the lights of Stonyford," he told her. He swung on to the lowest branch and began to climb. Without hesitating, she followed him.

"What's your name?" he asked, feeling cramped and cosy when she pushed against him on to a broad bough.

"Ellen Pender. My father's bought this place. We're going to build our new house here."

"No wonder she sounds like she owns the place," he thought. "She's a freeze-the-breeze." This was his mother's name for the inhabitants of Cypress Hill, who called the people from River View "blow-ins."

"Them ones up on the hill, they'd freeze the breeze with the snooty looks they give you," she complained, and the term had become part of the Hackett vocabulary.

Ben looked towards the old building, shrouded in the purple dusk of evening. "Will it be knocked down?" He suddenly felt sad. Despite its dereliction, Charney House kept its air of grandeur. It looked like an arrogant old lady who had seen better days as she gazed down upon the changing face of Stonyford.

"Oh yes. You'd hardly expect us to live in a dump like that!" Ellen waved her hand towards the house, casually dismissing its aged grandeur and its history.

The name Pender rang a bell in Ben's mind. When he looked down over the hill, the blurred shape of an enormous crane with tiny red lights embedded in its arm loomed out of the twilight. Suddenly her name clicked. PENDER'S LUXURY DEVELOPMENT. The signs were everywhere on Cypress Hill where luxurious new houses were being built. Her father was the property developer, David Pender. He was obviously a wealthy man, especially if he was able to buy Charney House.

"I was visiting that house down there." She leaned closer to Ben and pointed vaguely towards the hill where lights shone from the windows of houses. "That's where Douglas Barclaid lives. He's a creep."

"Why visit him then?"

"I went with my mother. Our parents are best friends. Pass the sick-bag, please!"

"He can't be that awful."

"If you like rats, he's not."

"Actually I do."

"You're kidding!"

He told her about Sheba and she shuddered. "I'm not surprised your mother freaked. I hate rats!"

"They're really lovely creatures. Look! I have one in my pocket. You can hold him if you like."

Her scream reminded him of his mother all those years ago. He had finally cracked Ellen Pender's cool. Climbing down the tree, she was as agile as a squirrel.

"You rotten punk!" she yelled, ducking from his grasp when he landed on the ground beside her and chased her around the tree. "You did that on purpose!" But she was laughing, eluding him and running through the bushes. Just as suddenly as she had appeared, she vanished so swiftly that he wondered if the magic of the old house had played tricks with his imagination.

"Ellen!" His voice echoed through the grounds and

was lost among the trees. Once he thought he saw a flash of white but it was only a plastic bag from Campion's, one of the supermarkets in the village. Dead leaves crunched beneath his feet. When he kicked them, they went soaring into the air like a flock of rust-covered birds on crumpled-tissue wings. The evening sounds had grown muffled when he left the grounds of the old house. Even the screeching of rooks in the trees sounded softer. A mist had risen from the damp grass and the breeze made whispering noises in the branches.

*

On the day that Charney House was demolished, Ben raced up Cypress Hill after school ended. Girls and boys from River View had already gathered, screaming with excitement when a huge ball of iron, swinging from a crane, smashed against the building. The walls seemed to shudder once. Then the house fell without a fight. Afterwards there was an eerie silence. The rubble settled and Charney House, which had stood for centuries watching over Cypress Hill and the village that nestled underneath, now seemed like just a heap of dusty bones.

3

A Stray on the Wastelands

Two years had passed since the Hackett family moved to Stonyford. Mr Hackett was working in an electronics factory on Four-Mile Industrial Estate and Mrs Hackett had given birth to her sixth child, a daughter called Maria. Ben and Cindy attended River View Comprehensive, a one-storey building overlooking the river. Mr Moone had not returned to his family and Mrs Moone, when she mentioned his name, spoke about him in the past tense. Danny never spoke about him at all. Susie and Cindy had formed a girls' soccer team. They took their name from the old house that used to stand on the hill and were known as the Charney Champs. A group of parents, led by Mrs Moone, tamed and flattened a wild section of the wastelands into a football pitch for them.

Ben and Danny sometimes walked to and from school together, just like old times. But the silence between them, once as relaxed as their conversation, was strained. When Mappo and his brother Billy joined the cider gang, they called for Danny in the evenings. Ben was never asked to go along. Without anything being said, Ben discovered that he was on the outside, looking on. It was a lonely feeling, watching a warm and comfortable friendship that he had taken for granted sliding away.

He made a new friend, Craigy the blacksmith, who still worked at his forge. Craigy was a wizened seventy-year-old with a scrunched-up mahogany face, a leather apron and a grip as strong as a champion arm-wrestler. Ben never saw him without a peaked cap pushed to the back of his head. In Stonyford Village, the old shops with their dusty interiors were gradually being replaced by shopping centres, fast food restaurants and video libraries. But Forge Alley seemed to belong to another age, far removed from the plastic and chrome of Trudy's Wonderburgers and the bright aisles of the supermarkets. With its distinctive horseshoe-shaped entrance, it was the only building in a narrow side-street at the end of the village. The forge was kept going by the two riding schools in Stonyford and by the young people from Cypress Hill, who brought their ponies to be shod. The blacksmith was renowned for his vetting skills. His experienced glance could immediately detect an injury or infection in a horse or pony. He lent Ben his books about horses and allowed him to help in the forge.

Danny stayed with the cider gang and in the morning there were dark shadows under his eyes, like the scorched circles of grass on the wastelands. Mrs Moone worried about her son. Ben grew to dread her knock on his front door and her request that he find Danny and bring him home. The gang would watch him approach and he would feel the sense of restlessness that came from them, like a taut wire that could snap at any moment. He would hear their laughter, loud and impulsive. Then, in a sudden change of mood, their voices would become angry, the words slurring when they argued with each other, flames throwing flickering shadows over the grass. Occasionally, Danny would be playing his mouth-organ. The loneliness of the sound shivered in the night.

"Piss off, Ben," was the only reply Danny ever made. Sometimes he went home with Ben. Sometimes he stayed by the bonfires.

It was on such a night that Ben saw the biker and the pony. Mrs Moone had called, twisting her hands together apologetically. "Just bring him home, Ben. Don't take any notice of what he says."

He left River View Avenue and walked across the stretch of wasteland that sloped towards the river. He saw the flames of a bonfire. From the river road on the opposite bank, he heard the roar of a motorbike as it climbed the blind bridge. The biker paid no attention to the red traffic light. But the bridge was free of traffic and the bike sped smoothly over the hump, the front wheel poised for an instant in mid-air. At the foot of the blind bridge, the biker turned off the road leading towards River View and entered the wastelands where hidden hollows and high mounds of earth were covered with thick, long grass.

As the bike flashed past, Ben saw a black leather-clad figure, tensed over the handlebars. There was something so aggressive about the revving sound of the engine that he felt a surge of anger. But he moved quickly out of the way. The biker circled the bonfire, taunting the cider gang and riding out of range before they could catch him. Sparks scattered into the darkness and an empty cider bottle sailed over his head. The biker passed Ben once again before crossing back over the blind bridge.

The headlight fanned the narrow river road then disappeared into the darkness of Clemartin's Stretch.

So intent was Ben on watching the biker that he did not notice the pony lumbering towards him. For an instant he thought it was his mind playing moon tricks. But he soon realised that this was a real live pony with a white star on his forehead and a coat that looked like it had been invaded by an army of moths.

The pony stopped, bent his head and began to nibble at the grass. His mane was clotted and dusty, a dull brown. He reminded Ben of a pony called Tippling Tom, owned by Trev Shaw, a scrap collector who had lived in Wheatfield Flats. A makeshift stable behind the flats was Tippling Tom's home and whenever Trev left him outside his local pub, the pony would whinny impatiently and rattle his harness until Trev came back out with a foaming glass of Guinness for him to drink. Ben had learned to ride Tippling Tom when he was ten years old.

Every time the women from the flats had seen him trotting the pony around the cement garden as if it was a competition arena at the Dublin Horse Show, they leaned over their balconies and whistled at him.

Ben had a packet of extra-strong peppermints in the pocket of his jeans. The pony eagerly took a sweet. He lifted his head and nuzzled the boy's hand, demanding more. Soon he had finished the packet. Even the wrapping paper disappeared down his throat before Ben could pull it free.

To own his own horse; that was Ben's dream. His horse would be a sleek smooth machine like the champion, White Heat, a famous Irish racehorse that was renowned internationally for his plucky spirit and his speed. Ben dreamed of a champion but, as his mother said, he was full of daft loving and when it spilled out over the skinny, knock-kneed, burnt-out pony standing so patiently beside him, White Heat was forgotten.

Ben's legs straddled the hard back. Soon his body adjusted to the rippling movements beneath him. The pony plodded towards the bonfire. "What do I do with you now?" Ben asked, gripping the brown mane. The pony was obviously a stray. Perhaps he belonged to one of the travelling families who sometimes camped on the wastelands. He had seen a family there last week but they had moved on the previous day. It was possible that they had forgotten the pony. He wondered what would happen if he suggested keeping the animal in the back garden of his house.

Mr Hackett had started planting vegetables in the top half but the bottom patch was still wild. Ben could build a stable there. The wastelands were no place for a stray. He was sure his mother would understand.

Danny was playing cards beside a fire fuelled by planks of wood that the gang collected each evening from the building sites.

"Don't you know anything, Hackett?" he shouted. "That pony belongs to Main Man McMullen. He'll break your legs in two if he sees you on it."

"That's for sure," said Mappo. He laughed abruptly. "My brother Billy can tell you all about that."

"He doesn't frighten me." Ben kept his voice steady. But he kept moving in case they could see his legs shaking. The pony, as if sensing his change of mood, whinnied uneasily. Main Man McMullen! How could he have forgotten? The first person he had been warned about when he moved to River View was the horse-dealer who lived in one of the old cottages on Highfern Row, on the far bank of Four-Mile River.

The eight cottages had been owned by old people whose lives had previously been disturbed only by the rippling journey of the river, and the bleating of sheep grazing on Clemartin's Stretch. But with the building of River View, they were unable to cope with the changes, the noise and the traffic, the children who swarmed over the blind bridge and into their gardens, robbing the fruit from their apple trees and sometimes setting fire to their hedges. One by one they were persuaded to sell their cottages to Main Man. Only Cathy Dill, who owned the end cottage, refused to sell. The children called her Batty Catty and said she was a witch. Her numerous cats were a familiar sight, swarming over her garden or dozing on the blind bridge.

As soon as he had bought the cottages, the horse-dealer knocked down the fences and hedges between the long gardens. They became a grazing area for his horses. A hedge, strengthened with wire, surrounded the back and front gardens. But it was easy for the animals to break out and wander over the blind bridge. Mr Hackett complained about them roaming around River View, ploughing up newly spread lawns or startling night drivers when they loomed suddenly in front of speeding cars. Even the cider gang accepted that the horse-dealer's animals were not to be touched. This lesson had been brought home to them last month when Billy Deane stole one of Main Man's horses, a mare that had only recently foaled. Main Man had been drinking in the Stony Arms when it happened. Billy had also been drinking on the wastelands and was as high as a kite on cider. He galloped the mare up Cypress Hill, shouting and waving an imaginary lasso. It was dawn before the mare was abandoned and left to roam the hilly roads.

She had developed a limp and her left eye-socket was torn when Main Man eventually found her.

Billy was terrified when he sobered up. He stayed indoors for a week. When he believed the fuss had died down, he was back on the streets again, lounging up against the wall of Trudy's Wonderburgers. Three days later he was discovered on a patch of wasteland with his leg fractured and his left eye swollen like a ripe plum. When the police called around to try to find out who was responsible, the teenagers on River View shook their heads and wouldn't say a word.

Ben slid clumsily from the pony's back and led him back over the blind bridge, moving quickly towards the cottages that squatted, almost hidden from view, behind overgrown hedges and trees. No lights glowed in the cottage that Main Man used as his home. A gap in the hedge, fresh and recently trampled, was obviously the pony's escape route. Dead twigs snapped beneath his hooves when Ben guided him through the hedge.

A number of horses stood perfectly still, blurred shapes in the gloom, loosely tethered to stakes that Main Man had hammered into the ground. Ben found a rope and secured the stray to an empty stake. The moon was like an orange, huge and shadowy. It seemed to hang above the garden, close enough to touch. Ben moved among the horses, stroking them, talking to them. They whinnied softly in reply and pushed their noses against his hand. They were gentle animals, mostly past their prime.

Some had a tough cut about them, reminding him once again of Tippling Tom. They were beasts of burden who had spent their lives trotting unheeded in front of frustrated city drivers, pulling heavy carts loaded with scrap-iron or coal. Sleek and well-fed ponies also grazed alongside them, but their ears flopped dejectedly.

When a hand grabbed Ben's sweatshirt, it was too late to duck out of the way. Main Man McMullen had a red face, pitted with scars that puckered his cheeks and dragged his left eye into a slit. His right eye was missing, the space covered by a black patch. The smell of whiskey was strong on his breath. When Main Man was not buying and selling horses, he spent most of his time drinking in the Stony Arms. "What the hell are you doing on my property, you young pup?" he growled. Ben tried to wriggle from his grip but it bit into the bones of his shoulder.

"I'm...ah...so...sorry Mr McMullen. I found that pony on the wastelands..." Main Man's grip tightened. "And I was just bringing him back to you."

Even though he was terrified of Main Man, Ben was also angry, hating the smell of neglect that hung over the gardens, the horse dung that was never swept up, the way the animals hung their heads, their ears flattened with weariness. It opened up some kind of wound in him. He pushed Main Man away and the burly man was so startled that he stepped backwards.

"Your animals are always roaming off and if you don't watch it, they'll be killed one of these nights. Or they'll cause an accident and then you'll be in real trouble. You shouldn't keep animals if you can't look after them properly!" He had not meant to shout. But the suffering he sensed in the animals, the nearness of Main Man, the whiskey fumes on his breath, his dirty hands, everything about him made Ben want to lash out.

"Ah ha! A pup who's prepared to cheek Main Man. Well, well, well!" Main Man laughed and spat on the ground. "Come over to the hedges till we see if there's any truth in your talk about this animal escaping. If I find out you're telling me lies, I'll give you such a hiding that you'll not be wearing tight pants again until you're eighty-five years old."

He inspected the trampled hedging, scratching his chin. Then, roughly, he shoved Ben through the gap. "Get going, fast, before I change my mind and give you that hiding, anyway. That's the only way to keep pups like you in line."

Ben sprinted along the river road, over the blind bridge and through the wastelands. He did not look behind him once or stop running until he reached his home.

4

Ben Delivers a Birthday Present

The pony continued to break out from Highfern Row. Sometimes other horses followed him. Main Man used planks of wood and rusting wire bases from beds to fix the gaps in the hedges. But, sooner or later, Ben would find the pony on the wastelands and, afraid that he might stumble and break a leg, he would shoo him back through the gap. The pony greeted the boy with low-pitched neighing sounds of pleasure, his droopy ears pricking up, his tail flicking in excitement when he saw him.

"Main Man was telling me about that pony," said Craigy. "He's called Jip and he's a restless sort of a creature, always trying to break free. The dealer's having a hard job selling him and he was wondering if I knew anyone who might be interested. He's asking too much for him, that's the problem. Main Man's a greedy sort, and vicious too, if the mood takes him. Keep well away from him. I heard on the grapevine that he's losing a lot of money on the gambling and that Murty Slomes is after him."

Murty Slomes was a moneylender, hated and feared

and needed by many people on River View, where unemployment was becoming a problem. A number of companies on Four-Mile Industrial Estate had not made the profits they had projected and there had been some closures and lay-offs.

When his summer school holidays started, Ben spent his free time with Craigy, learning farrier skills, not just shoeing horses, but also gaining knowledge of how to vet an animal, to check for hidden inflammations and injuries. He was an excellent student, his natural instincts reinforced by Craigy's expert knowledge.

One afternoon in July, Ben arrived at the forge and saw Main Man's large horse-box, with his white van attached to it, almost blocking the narrow street. A sleek black limousine was parked in front of the van. In the driving seat, a chauffeur in a peaked cap read the racing page of a newspaper.

"Come on in, lad," ordered Craigy, when he saw Ben at the entrance. "I'm just checking this mare for Mr Pender."

Main Man grunted at Ben. The man who stood beside him nodded abruptly and immediately turned his attention back to a black horse. Ben had forgotten what Ellen Pender looked like, yet her face came before his mind as soon as he saw her father. They were very alike, the same wide-spaced blue eyes, strong chin and black hair. Even though Mr Pender was of short, stocky build, and Main Man, looking more bedraggled than usual, towered above him, it was Mr Pender's presence that dominated the forge.

Craigy inspected every part of the mare, paying particular attention to her teeth and legs.

"I told you she was a beauty," Main Man said to Mr Pender when the blacksmith gave the mare a clean bill of health. "Your daughter couldn't ask for a better birthday present."

"You know your business, McMullen. But I don't take chances, no matter what the odds." Mr Pender glanced at his watch. He did not look hurried. Yet he had a brisk way about him, as if he lived his life on a time schedule. "I want this to be a surprise for Ellen, so have the horse delivered to Fairview Heights within the next hour. We've planned a small birthday presentation with some friends."

"Not to worry, sir. I'll take care of everything. You can always leave it to Main Man. I'll not see you stuck."

Mr Pender's face was expressionless when he looked at the dealer. "No one ever sees me stuck, McMullen. If they do, they soon find out that I am not pleased."

Main Man acknowledged the words by touching his forehead with his index finger. He was so servile it was difficult for Ben to recognise him as the same person who had bullied him that night on Highfern Row. A smile like oil slid across the dealer's lips when he listened to the purr of the limousine turning out of Forge Alley.

Ben watched the black mare pulling against Main Man, who was loading her into the horse-box. She was very different from the tired animals that he had seen in Main Man's garden. But Craigy had told him that the dealer was recognised as an expert on good horse-flesh. Despite his shady reputation, he was often asked to buy expensive ponies, for the young people who lived on Cypress Hill. These ponies were normally delivered to their new owners immediately and did not have to endure the cramped conditions in the gardens of Highfern Row.

"How much did that horse cost?" Ben asked.

"£3,000, at a rough guess," replied the blacksmith.

"£3,000 for a birthday present!" Ben could not believe his ears. It was impossible to imagine so much money, let alone using it to buy a birthday present. Five years previously, before his grandmother died, she had given him his first sum of money, two hundred pounds deposited in a post office account. He had considered this to be a vast amount of money. "I'm giving you your legacy before I die, Ben," she told him, her thin shape barely visible under the bedclothes. She smelled of medicine and cigarette smoke, a sick old woman, who would die a week later. "That's for when you're older and you have a few pounds of your own to add to it. And remember this—I want to see it multiplying, not dividing. Whether I'm up in that place above or the one below, I'll be keeping a close watch on you. Since then his mother had refused to allow him to touch it, but, looking at the black mare, its value suddenly seemed deflated.

Main Man switched on the engine of his van. It whined and coughed, then fell silent. The horse-dealer opened the bonnet and cursed loudly. Craigy and Ben hovered around the van, offering advice to the back of Main Man's head.

The horse whinnied, shrill nervous blasts of sound that added to Main Man's fury.

"I've got to get the animal over to the Heights on time or Pender will breathe acid down my neck!" He roared at his van but, refusing to be intimidated, it coughed once, then settled into silence again.

"I'll ride the horse over," Ben offered. "I know where the place is."

Main Man considered this alternative to an acid neck-wash. "You must be joking! I'm not putting this expensive piece of horse-flesh in the hands of a horse thief," he jeered. "You river rats would steal the snot from a man's nose while he was blowing it."

"Suit yourself!" snapped Ben. He hated the term "river rats" and often heard it used to describe the cider gang. He stormed back into the forge where yellowing horse charts were pinned to the walls. Boxes of clips and nails and the tools of Craigy's trade were cluttered together on a smoke-stained workbench. From the entrance Ben grimly watched Main Man's renewed attempts to start the van. At last the dealer admitted defeat.

"OK, pup. Now's your chance to ride a real champion. Slap a saddle on the beast, Craigy. Pender's groom can bring it back to you later."

"I think Ben has withdrawn his offer." Craigy's eyes twinkled. He surveyed the boy's flushed face and winked. "Maybe if you make it worth his while he could be persuaded to change his mind. I'd say now, if you offered him twenty-five pounds, he might be prepared to oblige."

Ben kept his sullen expression with great difficulty.

"Twenty-five pounds! For what? Riding a horse to the top of the hill?" roared Main Man.

"Oh dear me! Look at the time! The Pender birthday party will be getting underway very soon now," said Craigy, examining a non-existent watch.

"All right! All right!" snarled Main Man. "I'll give him the money when he returns."

"Now, McMullen. He gets it now!" snapped Craigy. The humour had left his face. Main Man fumed and peeled off five five-pound notes, slapping them into Ben's willing palm. "No galloping her. If I hear that the horse was delivered in a lather of sweat, you're for the high jump. Understand, pup!"

On the summit of Cypress Hill, Ben rode the horse along Sallin's Lane, a narrow trail that curved around the back of the grounds of Mr Pender's house. Trees on each side of the lane framed them in a leafy arch. "Fairview Heights" was written in fancy lettering on a gate name-plate and Ben turned in through the gateway.

The groom was waiting. "Where's Main Man? What the hell happened? Here, give me the animal till I get her ready." He barely listened to Ben's explanations, hurriedly brushing the horse until her black coat, already gleaming, seemed to shimmer with health and energy.

Ben prepared to leave. "See you, girl." He stroked the horse's neck, allowing her to dribble over his fingers when he slipped a peppermint into her mouth. He felt sad when he looked around the tidy grounds. Only the chestnut trees reminded him of that night when he had explored Charney House for the last time. Everything else had changed, even the name of the house. Apart from the hedging on Sallin's Lane, it was surrounded by an expensive, mock-antique stone wall. The dried-up lake-bed had been filled with water. It looked exactly as he had imagined, the water reflecting reeds and water-lily leaves. Two swans, trailing half-grown cygnets, lazily drifted past a small summer-house with a high-domed glass roof and a patio overlooking the lake.

He moved to the front of the house, keeping out of

sight behind dense clumps of rhododendrons. The groom led the black mare towards a flag-stoned courtyard. A flight of steps led up to the open double-doors. From where he stood, Ben could see into the hall. It gleamed with a woody mellow light. Suddenly Mr Pender appeared, his hands across his daughter's eyes, carefully leading her down the steps.

"Come with me, my birthday girl," he said. "Steady now, we're going down the steps. One at a time, that's right, we can't allow anything to happen to the birthday girl."

In the middle of the courtyard he removed his hands from around her eyes. "Happy fourteenth birthday, darling."

Ellen Pender blinked. Then her eyes rested with astonishment on the slender mare with the black coat. "She can't be mine. Oh Daddy. I can't believe it." Her voice was a shriek of pleasure. "She's glorious, wonderful, magnificent. I love you…love you…love you!"

When the hugging and kissing had died down, she began to examine the mare. "What's her name?"

"Dark Sprite. I thought it was an apt name. With you on her back, Ellen, she'll fly faster than the darkest fairy spirit."

The groom had discreetly left as soon as Mr Pender appeared, leaving Ellen to soothe the mare, who was darting nervous glances around the courtyard. Her father gave a discreet glance at his watch.

"Am I keeping you from something important, Daddy?" she asked. Ben immediately picked up the anxiety in her voice.

Her father shook his head. "It's your day, Ellen. Big

business can stand still long enough to celebrate it."

"You've probably cancelled something very important to be with me. Thank you." She buried her face in the mare's neck. "I really am the luckiest girl in the world."

Ben felt sweaty and uncomfortable. The afternoon sun beat down on his head. He wanted to leave Fairview Heights but he was afraid to move from the shelter of the rhododendrons in case they saw him.

"Come on everyone, come and join us!" shouted Mr Pender.

"No need to shout, David. We are coming." A slim, well-dressed woman walked down the steps. Her cheek was extended graciously towards Ellen, who obediently kissed it. It looked cool and soft like a peach. She was followed by another couple, and a boy who looked about a year older than Ellen. A butler took up the rear, gliding behind them with a silver tray which carried six long-stemmed glasses and a bottle of champagne in an icebucket.

"Happy birthday, darling. I hope you realise what a lucky young lady you are? Have you said 'thank you' properly to your father?" asked the woman who had first appeared.

"Of course I have, Mummy!" There was a note of impatience in Ellen's voice.

The others must be friends of the family, possibly the people Ellen had mentioned when he met her in the old house. Ben could not remember their name. The boy was tall with a long face and brown wavy hair swept back from his high forehead. There was a haughty air about him, a bored expression on his face. Ben disliked him on sight. He did not try to understand his reaction but he knew it as a feeling that would never change. Then he dismissed him from his mind.

The butler stood silently in the background while Mr Pender uncorked the champagne. The sparkling wine spilled free in a froth of bubbles. He held it towards the mare for an instant before filling the six glasses.

"I hereby christen you Dark Sprite. Now let us drink to your future with the Pender family."

"I do not think you should let her drink, David!" Mrs Pender's voice was soft but insistent when Ellen was handed a glass, half-full of champagne.

"Nonsense! A little drop. That's all I'm giving her. Just enough to wet her lips on this special day. Don't fuss, Audrey. Cheers, my birthday girl!"

Ben could not help grinning as he watched the scene in front of him. Whenever any of the Hacketts had a birthday, they got clothes for their presents and their mother dashed to the local newsagent at the last minute to buy a card with a verse that made the child in question sound like a paragon of virtue. Mrs Hackett obviously thought so too for she normally put an X through the soppy verse and wrote "Lies—all lies. But I love you anyway!" Then she served them slices of birthday cake, oozing cream and jam and with thick icing, which always made them feel slightly ill.

Mr Pender made a short speech and there was an air of finality about him when he briskly drained his glass of champagne and replaced it on the tray. "I'm afraid I must go, Ellen. I'll see you later this evening in time for your party."

It was the decisive tone that he had used at the forge.

"You won't be late, Daddy? Promise!"

"Of course not. Don't worry. I'll be there."

Ellen stroked Dark Sprite's nose and watched her father stride across the flag-stoned courtyard. The chauffeur started the car. The engine purred like a well-fed cat and the black limousine glided down the driveway of Fairview Heights. When Ellen turned around her expression was blank, just for an instant, but long enough for it to register on Ben's mind.

He slipped quietly away, heading back towards the shelter of Sallin's Lane. It was only after he crossed the blind bridge and was walking through a patch of wasteland that her expression stopped pulling at his memory. When Danny Moone's face looked like that, Ben knew that he was thinking about his father, and wondering when he would return. He shook his head at the ridiculousness of such a comparison.

Main Man's notes crackled in his pockets. There was a satisfying sound to them. He would treat himself to lunch at Trudy's Wonderburgers and, afterwards, go to the cinema. Maybe Danny would come with him. Twenty-five pounds might not buy a horse but he was going to have a lot of time discovering just how far it could be stretched.

5

A Visit to Downshandon Market

Downshandon Market was reached by passing through Forge Alley. It was an old-fashioned square used by traders on Sundays to sell hand-made jewellery, clothes and second-hand books from their stalls. But Craigy often talked about the old days when the horse fair at Downshandon Market lasted for a week in August and people came from hundreds of miles away to attend it. There used to be music and drinking in the pubs, dancing in the streets and horse-racing on Clemartin's Stretch. Over the years, the horse fair had lost its popularity and although it was still held on one Saturday in the middle of August it was a quiet event compared to the wild, wonderful times that Craigy described. When the date for the event drew near, Craigy and Ben agreed to visit it together. When Danny heard about the horse fair, he asked Ben if he could go as well.

"At least it'd be something to do in this kip," he muttered.

Four months previously, a letter had arrived for Danny from his father. He had been living in England but was returning to Ireland and intended visiting his family in Stonyford the following week. No further word had been heard from him. Danny never told anyone about the letter but Mrs Moone told Mrs Hackett that she had found it under Danny's pillow, torn in pieces and stuck back together again with sticky-tape.

On the night before the fair, Ben was sent to the wastelands to find him. He had fallen asleep by the bonfire. When Ben lifted him and draped Danny's limp arm around his neck, the smaller boy staggered and slumped against him. It was the first time Ben had ever seen him drunk.

"Hold on, Danny. We're nearly home," he said, every time the smaller boy moaned against his shoulder.

Ben had not believed that Danny would remember the arrangement to go to Downshandon Market but when he was leaving the following morning, the Moones' front door opened and Danny appeared. Despite red-veined eyes and an unhealthy grey pallor, he was ready for action. He looked older than his fifteen years, his face buried in the hood of his sweatshirt, his forehead anxiously puckered into premature lines.

When the boys crossed the blind bridge, they saw two large horse-boxes outside Highfern Row. The dealer and another man were coaxing horses into them.

Downshandon Market opened up a world of strange noises to Ben. He listened to the clattering hooves and whinnying horses, the harsh sounds of men bargaining, a hand firmly slapping the rump of a pony, the deals struck as horses changed hands in a fencing match of lies and banter. Children in knee-high riding boots and skin-tight jeans gazed with adoring eyes at plump ponies and spoke persuasively to their parents.

After one astonished look around him, Danny appeared revolted by his surroundings. He drew in his breath in exaggerated gasps of irritation, wrinkled up his nose and scowled at the horses, as if they were his personal enemies.

Craigy knew everyone. He was welcomed and thumped on his arm by beefy-looking men with red faces. Women spoke to him in clipped accents and asked his advice about the horses they were hoping to buy. Main Man McMullen moved among the sellers and buyers with a swaying gait, his left eye slitted with knowledge of everything that was going on. When he saw Ben, he gave no sign of recognition. He brought a prospective buyer to view one of his horses. The mare had a shiny coat and she was bright-eyed, high-tailed and frisky. Her hooves pranced on the cobblestones.

"Cosmetic surgery," snorted Craigy, furiously. "I'd recognise one of Main Man's figged horses a mile away!" Figging, he explained to Danny, meant that a dishonest owner had shoved a lump of tobacco or ginger up the tail of a horse that was past its prime. The discomfort this created caused the horse to jump about like a lively young colt, behaviour that often fooled an inexperienced buyer. Danny looked interested for the first time since his arrival. He wandered off with Craigy to view the rest of Main Man's horses.

Jip had been separated from the other horses. When Ben saw him, his heart seemed to fold over with pain. The pony's eyes were closed and he fidgeted uneasily. He heard Ben's voice and lifted his head in welcome, eyes opening, ears pricked. He had nice eyes, like almonds. His brown mane was no longer dusty and matted-looking.

"You've been spruced up for the beauty parade," Ben muttered, feeling such a wave of affection for the skinny old hack that he put his arms around Jip's neck.

"I can see you're fond of that pony, pup." Main Man had been watching them. "He's not a bad bit of horseflesh." He slapped Jip's flank. The pony jerked his head and his front hooves did a jittery little dance. He was frightened of Main Man, twisting his neck in different directions, trying to get as far away as possible from the dealer.

"Do you want to make an offer for him?"

"You must be joking," Ben replied. "Where would I get the money for a horse."

"You might, if the price was right."

Ben hesitated, thinking about his grandmother's legacy. In fact, he had been thinking about nothing else since he arrived at Downshandon Market. Main Man had no difficulty reading Ben's thoughts. The boy's fair skin was flushed with excitement, his hand scratched his head nervously. He squinted, trying to outstare the dealer, but he was not able to hide the excited gleam in his hazel eyes. The dealer's hand stroked Jip's back in an absent-minded gesture as if his thoughts were elsewhere.

"Too bad you're not interested. Not that I blame you. This fellow's too fond of breaking loose and causing trouble, as you should know. It's the dog-can for him and I'll be glad to get rid of him."

Ben knew what he meant. Canine Chops was a dog-food processing plant in the industrial estate. Danny said they made mincemeat out of dead horses to be sold as dog food. "You wouldn't sell him for dog food!" Ben stared from Jip to Main Man, horrified at the idea.

"Why not?" growled the dealer. "The best price I've been offered so far for him came from Taggy Somers over at Canine Chops. It's not a luxury four-star hotel I'm running on Highfern Row."

"You can't do that," Ben repeated, his voice rising. Jip seemed to quiver, as if he understood what Main Man was saying. "Why can't you sell him to someone else?"

"Watch my lips move, pup. No one else is interested. I've got a fair price from Somers. End of story."

Taggy Somers was making his way towards them.

"Name your price!" Ben demanded.

Main Man snorted with laughter. "I thought you had no money. What are you offering? Lollipop sticks!"

His contemptuous tone infuriated Ben. "I've money saved. I could take it out of the post office on Monday, if I wanted to."

"OK! £300! Not a penny less."

"£200! In cash. Not a penny more." He felt as if he had pitched himself into a deep, dark well. Taggy Somers had stopped to speak to someone. Nervously, Ben argued with Main Man, trying to keep his voice deep and steady.

"Huh! Chickenfeed. Taggy Somers has offered me more!" said Main Man.

Ben called his bluff and refused to budge from his offer.

"You'll have to match his price, at least," demanded Main Man.

Taggy was moving towards them again.

"I haven't got any more!" The desperation in Ben's cry must have convinced Main Man. Suddenly he gave a sigh of defeat, slapped the boy's palm and agreed.

"You're only a runt, but you're as hard as nails," he

growled. "You're getting a bargain, make no mistake about it. Have that money over to Highfern Row as soon as the post office opens on Monday. Are you hearing me, pup? Monday! Or I'll be down in River View looking for you. Savvy? You can take the pony away with you then." He began talking to another man, ignoring Ben, who walked slowly away, his head bent. He bumped into Taggy Somers.

"Hey! Watch where you're going." He was a small man with a body like a barrel, a bullet-shaped head and a neck as thick and knotty as a tree trunk.

"That's one pony that won't go through your mincing machine," Ben snapped, pointing back towards Jip.

"What the hell are you talking about?" demanded Taggy.

"That pony you were going to buy for Canine Chops. Main Man's just sold him to me."

"Is that a fact now?" Taggy started to laugh. "Listen kid. I wouldn't offer tuppence for that sorry-looking bag of bones. I don't know what you've paid but, whatever it is, I'll guarantee that it's one hundred per cent too much."

With a patronising pat on the boy's shoulder, he moved on. Ben Hackett, first-time pony owner, stood alone, surrounded by the clattering, shouting, bargaining sounds of Downshandon Market and knew that he would hear Taggy Somers' laughter for a long time to come. Reality was not only all around him, it was also waiting for him at home. In his mind's eye he could see his mother's face. It was not a pleasant sight. He also imagined his grandmother sitting on a cloud (probably *a cloud of cigarette smoke rather than one of angelic* origin) screwing up her wrinkled skin in disapproval over the casual way he had disposed of her legacy.

The enormity of what he had done made him feel ill. He had a pony. But he had no stable, saddle, bridle, harness or food for him. All he had was a pool of love and it seemed very little as he walked home and wondered what on earth he was going to say to his mother.

6

The Conversion of Mrs Hackett

The houses of River View seemed to close around Ben. Children ran from all directions and followed him, cheering wildly.

"Hey Ben! You up there on the donkey! Give us a ride," Susie Moone shouted when he turned into River View Avenue. She screeched with laughter, looking up at him with her bold brown eyes. Susie's romantic relationship with Ben had never moved beyond that "moone-struck" night in Wheatfield Flats. The girls' football team, which she managed, was her only passion in life. The Champs were training in Susie's front garden when they saw Jip. With shrieks of glee, they followed their manager and crowded around him. Ben groaned. He tried to look dignified when Susie crouched in a goalkeeper stance in front of the pony.

"Hey, Danny! Would you ever come and have a look at Ben Hackett," she shouted to her brother, who was sitting on his garden wall. "He thinks he's a yuppie sitting on his ass!"

The Charney Champs thought this was hilarious.

"He always was a yuppie asshole," growled Danny. He

pulled deeply on the end of a cigarette and flicked the butt towards Jip's hooves.

Susie Moone ducked behind Jip. She tried to pull his tail, then ran back to the Champs, shrieking at the top of her voice, when Jip lifted his tail into a magnificent arch and crapped over the centre of the road.

The Champs screeched with laughter. Mrs Hackett waited, watching, arms on her hips, daring her son to bring the pony in through the gateway. Jip came to a stop, looming in front of 16 River View Avenue. He seemed to shrink the doorway into a little sliver through which he would never be able to enter.

Ben dismounted. "Hi Ma. What do you think? I've bought a pony. What're the chances of bringing him into the back garden?

"About the same as the man in the moon has of coming down and jiving on our kitchen table," she replied. Her eyes reminded Ben of icebergs.

He wilted before her gaze. "Ah Ma! I swear to God he'll be no trouble. I'll look after him and exercise him on the wastelands and feed him...and everything..."

"Would you mind telling me how we're supposed to get this creature into the back garden?" demanded Mrs Hackett. "Has it escaped your attention that we live in a terraced house?"

"There's no reason why I can't bring him in through the hall door."

Mrs Hackett's face turned pale. "You're not bringing that monster through my house." Her eyes bulged when Jip whinnied, a shrill burst of sound through quivering nostrils as if to say, "Stop all this nonsense and let me through immediately."

When it came to verbal exchanges, Mrs Hackett was a match for anyone. "Just you shut up, you mangy bag of bones," she shrieked.

The Charney Champs, led by Susie, sat on Hacketts' garden wall, legs dangling on each side, elbows tucked into their waists, jogging their bodies up and down and making horsy noises. Ben stared pleadingly at his mother through a thick fringe of straw-coloured hair, bleached by the sun.

"And how did you manage to afford a pony, if that's not too personal a question to ask?" she demanded.

"You know that little bit of money Gran left me?"

"Your legacy!" she screeched, as if he had defiled something sacred. "You've spent your legacy on that skeleton? Oh my God! Your legacy's gone!"

"Ma, it was only £200."

This caused her to shriek even louder. "May your granny's spirit haunt you forever. Take this animal out of my front garden at once. Burn it. Hang it. Bury it. Get it out of my sight!" She clipped him across his ear and refused to listen to his pleas, convinced that he was suffering from delusions of grandeur. "You want to look like them freeze-the-breezes up on Cypress Hill with their toy ponies, all dressed up in their fancy hats and boots!"

Then a miracle occurred. The most unpopular woman on River View, Mrs Toner, was an unlikely-looking miracle. She lived in the house on the other side of Hacketts, a fact that caused deep distress to Mrs Hackett. Mrs Toner had not come to River View from Wheatfield Flats and she believed that this gave her superior status in the neighbourhood.

"That one is as stuck up in the air as a seal's nose," Mrs Hackett would say, watching Mrs Toner polishing her patio glass doors or dusting the many ornaments that decorated all the windows of her house.

Mrs Toner opened her front door and glared out. "What is going on here?" she demanded in a clipped, precise accent.

"Ben Hackett's bought a new horse," shouted Susie, gleefully. "He's going to keep it in his back garden."

"He certainly is not!" snapped Mrs Toner. "I never heard of anything so utterly ridiculous."

"And what's it to you if he is?" demanded Mrs Hackett. She always put on a posh accent when she spoke to Mrs Toner. "If my son, Benjamin Hackett, wants to keep his pony in our back garden, who are you to say he can't?"

"There are those of us who did not come from a city centre slum and we would like to keep the tone of this neighbourhood up to a certain standard, Mrs Hackett."

"I don't notice you complaining about them young ones up on Cypress Hill. What about the horses in *their* back gardens."

"Allow me to correct you, Mrs Hackett." Mrs Toner's smile had all the charm of a worm-eaten apple. "They do not have back gardens. They have grounds. And their horses are stabled in those grounds. There is a subtle difference—even if you fail to notice it."

"Oh, I notice the difference all right, Mrs Toner. What you're saying is that there's one law for the nobs on Cypress Hill and one for the yobs on River View like me— and you."

Mrs Toner lifted her eyebrows. She looked at Mrs

Hackett down the length of her nose. Her face was flushed and angry.

"Just you try bringing a horse into River View Avenue and you will regret it. Do you understand me, Mrs Hackett."

"Don't you dare threaten me, you Snob Blob," yelled Ben's mother. "Anyway, it's a pony, so there!" She opened her front door as wide as possible.

The Charney Champs leapt up on the wall. They began to cheer and whistle, to sing the Charney Champs' team song. "We've won. we've won we've won we've won." Ben had never heard any other words to that song. Even when they lost their matches, they still marched home singing it. Susie said it was positive thinking.

Mrs Toner ordered them to "cease that idiotic caterwauling" and they sang louder. "Pony or horse, you haven't heard the last of this," she shouted. Ben could feel her fury, aimed at his mother like something hot and spiteful. There was a fanatical light in her eyes when she saw the rear view of the pony disappear through the hall door. Jip didn't help matters by flicking his tail at her before the door closed.

"Mind my ornaments. Oh, mind my Busy Lizzie ...he'll eat the leaves!" Mrs Hackett cried as the pony lumbered through the hall. "I'll murder you, Ben, for inflicting this animal on me!"

"It's just for a while, Ma." He tried to comfort her. "I can't leave him out on the wastelands. Anything could happen to him. Come on, Ma. You were great outside. A real champ!"

Mrs Hackett waved him away. "Chump more like it. And how are you going to afford to keep him, may I ask?"

"I'll get a job, a part-time job in the evenings and I'll give you all my wages."

"You! Work! You wouldn't know how to lift a cup to your lips if you were dying with thirst." She was unimpressed by her son's new-found determination. Ben made her a cup of tea and closed the kitchen window on Mrs Toner's voice.

"Do not dare look over my fence, you ignorant pony. We will see what happens when the horse pound comes around. They will remove you in their truck before you can flick your tail and that will be the end of your nasty little adventure. Oh yes! That will be the end of it!"

7

The Charney Champs Find a Mascot

When Mrs Hackett went shopping the following day, Ben brought Jip through the hall and out the front door without mishap. He rode to Forge Alley, where Craigy's eyes widened with surprise when Ben told him what he had done.

"You know I don't approve of keeping horses in confined spaces, lad. But you have the glad eye for animals and you'll treat him well." He did not tell Ben that he was a fool and, apart from shaking his head ruefully when he inspected Jip, he kept his thoughts to himself. Just as Ben was leaving, he handed him the saddle and bridle Ben had used when he delivered Dark Sprite to Ellen Pender. They were old, smelling of polish and horse sweat.

"Take them, Ben," said Craigy. "I have them since I was a lad. I always wanted to pass them on to someone who would love horses as much as I do. And call into Campion's Supermarket tomorrow. I'll have a word with the owner. I know he could do with a lad working part-time to stock the shelves. You're going to need money to feed that horse. He might look like an advertisement for a starvation diet, but I suspect he'll eat you out of house and home."

Jip settled without any problem into River View. His only crime was to eat the cabbages and lettuces that Mr Hackett had managed to coax from the stony soil of the back garden. As Mrs Hackett was suspicious of anything that appeared in her vegetable basket caked with clay and decorated with dangling roots she was secretly relieved to see the trampled vegetable patch. Even Mr Hackett took it calmly. "At least someone has the good sense to appreciate my hard work." He stared at his family of vegetable-haters. "If I had to wait for you lot to eat the fruits of my labours, I'd be an old man." He was tanned and fit from working in the garden each evening. He still sighed for the smell of the river Liffey but he was settling into River View and Cindy had persuaded him to join the Charney Champs Parents Committee. The committee kept the grass cut, the lines painted, the nets in order and cheered themselves silly every time the Charney Champs scored a goal.

To oblige his wife, Mr Hackett laid a roll of heavy plastic covering over the hall carpet and the Hackett family grew used to their mother's anxious shrieks when Jip was led through the kitchen. Within a week, Ben saw her feeding peppermints to the horse and holding Maria on his back while Jip obediently plodded around the garden. "Have you stabled our pony for the evening, Benjamin?" she would shout in her poshest accent every time Mrs Toner glared over the garden wall.

Jip's biggest fans were the Charney Champs. On Sunday afternoons, Cindy brought him to the football pitch on the wastelands. For about five minutes before their match, the Champs danced around the horse.

They wore a red and black strip with the name of their team printed in gold lettering on the back. Libby Smith had knitted Jip a scarf in the team colours. When the Champs did their warm-up dance, they stamped their feet, waved their hands skywards and sang their pre-match song in the most bloodcurdling voices. "We're gonna win...we're gonna win...you can bet your life we're gonna win!" Susie Moone was still working on the lyrics.

Then they watched Jip anxiously for his reaction. He always obliged them by tossing back his head and whinnying shrilly, a sound that made the Champs cheer and march off to victory. For it was a fact that they had not lost a match since Jip became their mascot. When the Champs were not knocking on Ben's front door demanding that Jip be brought down to the wastelands to rehearse their team song, they were hanging over Susie's garden wall, feeding him grass and apples and peppermints and sugar lumps.

Soon after their mascot's arrival in River View, they had helped Ben to build a stable. Late in the evening, planks of wood and bricks were delivered in wheelbarrows by the Champs.

"It's just stuff that Dad doesn't need any more," explained the Charney Champs' centre forward, Olive Bricken, whose father ran a small builders' supply yard in River View.

"In a pig's eye," said Mrs Hackett. She glared suspiciously at a pile of wooden planks. "Those girls are nicking the stuff from Bricken's yard. I'm sure of it."

"Nicking! Your mother said we were nicking!" cried

Olive, outraged and offended, when Ben told her what his mother suspected. "No way Ben. I nearly broke my neck in that yard last week with all those dirty old planks lying around. We're only doing Dad a favour by cleaning the place up for him." She stared at Ben with blue, innocent eyes and winked. "There's a load of roofing stuff that's been there for years. Dad's totally forgotten all about it. Honest. I'll see what I can do."

For a week they worked hard, building Jip's stable. Then one evening, Olive's father paid them a visit. As soon as he appeared at the Hacketts' kitchen door, his daughter vaulted the wall into Moones' garden and disappeared with a muttered, "This is where I get off the bus, Ben. See you around."

Mr Bricken's plump face turned puce when he looked at Jip's stable. A vein on his shining bald head began to throb. He turned to the silent group of teenagers and told them that he would have every one of them jailed for robbery for at least ten years, including his daughter when he caught up with her.

Mrs Hackett stood at the kitchen door moaning. "I knew it. I knew it. But no one ever listens to me. I'm just a skivvy around here!"

Then Jip ambled towards Mr Bricken and pushed his nose curiously into the builder's calloused hand. Mr Bricken ignored him. Jip rubbed his face against the dusty jacket, butted him, as if to say: "Hey! I like you, so pay attention to me."

"As for calling yourselves builders? I've seen infants build better than that with Lego bricks!" Mr Bricken's roar was beginning to lose its power. He began to stroke the white star on Jip's forehead. "That's not a bad animal,

Ben," he growled, after a few minutes. "I always wanted a horse when I was a boy. But we never had any room for one. I can see you're not letting a little problem like space stand in your way." His voice had suddenly gone soft with memory. "But you've got to do it right or don't bother doing it at all. I'll be back after I've had a few words with my daughter."

As punishment for being the ringleader, Olive Bricken had to work in her father's yard every Saturday for a month. She missed four Charney Champ matches and, when the team continued to win, she found it difficult to get her position back again. But Ben stayed very quiet when she ranted on about her father's inhumanity.

Instead of having Ben jailed for ten years, Mr Bricken returned the following evening to knock down the makeshift building. In no time at all, a fine red-brick stable was erected, with a half-door. The name JIP was painted in white letters above the doorway. Mrs Toner stared grimly down upon them from her bedroom window. Twice she had rung the pound and when the officer arrived on River View to check out her story of a wild horse eating tree trunks and savaging small children, Jip was nowhere to be found.

But she had vowed that she would not rest until she had disposed of that "disgusting, smelly, ferocious beast." "The evidence," she gloated. "At last I have evidence of the horse's existence."

Next day, Mr Slowey and his horse truck were seen approaching River View.

"The pound's on the way! The pound's on the way!" Like jungle drums, the Charney Champs passed the word around. Mrs Hackett had gone to bed with a headache when she heard the Charney Champs arriving with the news so it was Cindy, with baby Maria balanced on her hip, who opened the door to Mr Slowey. She escorted him out to Jip's stable where the Charney Champs were doing knee-stretches and sideways bends. They looked blankly at him. What was he talking about? A stable? No, this wasn't a stable. Couldn't he see that it was a training centre for the famous Charney Champs. Jip's scarf was draped like a banner over his name above the door. But Mr Slowey sniffed the pungent, horsy smell and asked the Champs if they thought he came up on the last bus and were they trying to tell him that this building did not house at least one animal?

"That's a terrible thing to call us, sir," replied Olive Bricken, jumping and trying to head an imaginary ball. "We've been called animals before. But only by the teams we beat."

Maria spoiled their show of innocence by stretching out her arms, calling "Yip! Yip!", making a loud whinnying noise, then weeping loudly when she realised her favourite pet was missing.

"This is not a knacker's yard. I demand the removal of that horse," shouted Mrs Toner from her back garden.

"I can't remove him if I can't find him," snapped Mr Slowey, who found her a very tiresome woman.

Before leaving Stonyford, Mr Slowey stopped off at Forge Alley. As he expected, he found a boy, the old blacksmith and a large, ungainly pony in the forge.

When the first houses on River View had been completed, stray horses had been a big problem on the wastelands. Craigy had formed a horse club and had taught the young owners how to groom their horses and look after their health. But, in the end, the horses had to go, and Mr Slowey became a regular and much-feared visitor on River View. He had been angered and disgusted at the way some of the young people injured and neglected the animals. But there were others, boys and girls who cared deeply for their horses, and he found it difficult to forget the anguish on their faces when their horses were brought to the pound and their young owners were not able to afford the charges to release them. That was many years ago and now, thought Mr Slowey, it looked as if the problem was starting again. Yet he knew that the boy staring so fearfully at him belonged to the latter group.

His experienced eyes inspected the pony for any signs of injury or cruelty. Unlike the best fairy stories, Jip had not undergone a transformation as soon as he began to receive some love and attention from the Hackett family. He was still the skinniest, ugliest-looking pony Mr Slowey had ever seen. But Jip was filled with contentment and this showed in the shine of his eyes and the sheen of his coat. Despite himself, Mr Slowey was impressed.

He ignored Ben and greeted the blacksmith. "There's a lot of complaints coming in to the pound from a woman called Mrs Toner over on River View. I don't know whether she's suffering from delusions but she says there's a horse being kept in a back garden of one of the houses."

"Is that a fact now?" said Craigy, intently inspecting Jip's hoof. "And did you find the animal in question?"

"No, I didn't. Although I did find a group of young madams who thought I'd scrambled my brains for breakfast. Did you ever come across them? They're called the Charney Champs."

"Now that you mention it, I think I've heard of them," replied Craigy.

Mr Slowey sighed. "The problem is, I can't ignore complaints about horses that cause trouble. So I might have to call back again. Maybe I'll find him the next time and maybe I won't. Ah well, that's life, I suppose. We're always chasing the elusive shadow. The problem is, what do we do with it when we find it?"

"He's always been a bit of a philosopher," said Craigy when Mr Slowey left. He gave a quiet growl of satisfaction. "But he's not a bad skin. I'd say he'll leave you alone unless there's real trouble. So keep a close eye on Jip and don't even look sideways at Mrs Toner."

8

Passage Rights Through Sallin's Lane

Ben rose early each morning to exercise Jip on Clemartin's Stretch before going to school. On Thursday and Friday evenings he worked from five until nine in Campion's. He also worked a full day on Saturday, leaving Cindy to lead Jip down to the wastelands to graze and bring good luck to the Champs. Ben still called into Craigy's forge. The two friends never tired talking about horses. If there was a racing report in the morning paper about White Heat, Ben would cut out the photograph of the champion streaking past the winning post.

"A White Heat groupie," Craigy called him. White Heat was a thoroughbred grey with a coat that gleamed like white satin. He was a natural star and enjoyed prancing and showing off before the television cameras. His strength was in his finish and the crowd went crazy with excitement each time he came from behind, effortlessly passing out the field until it looked as if the other horses were standing still. Ben's bedroom wall was covered with White Heat posters and photographs, and he was dropping broad hints to his mother that he wanted *In the Heat of the Moment*, the official White Heat biography, for Christmas.

But Christmas was still a long way off. October was warm, an Indian summer that burnished the leaves and made them reluctant to fall from the trees. In the mornings Ben rode his horse across the blind bridge, hurried him past Highfern Row and gave him his head on Clemartin's Stretch. He dreamed of White Heat, loved Jip, and planned a future filled with horses. The mist sat low over Four-Mile River, reflecting the sun when it edged across the horizon like a red wound in the sky. In the emptiness of Clemartin's Stretch he laughed out loud and declared that life was good—very good indeed.

Sometimes, in the distance, he would see Ellen Pender on her black mare. Once they rode past each other and she shouted "Morning," smiling at him, sharing the exhilaration of her morning gallop. It was obvious that she did not recognise him. That was not surprising. Since his fifteenth birthday, Ben's mother said, he was growing like a runner bean. Last week his Aunt Shirley, a giddy, giggly woman who wore bright red lipstick and denim shorts with frills on the legs, had kissed him and shrieked: "Uhhhh! You've got stubble, Ben," as if the few hairs on his chin would give her some sort of disease. Ellen had also changed. He had noticed it at Fairview Heights but, up close, it was more apparent. Her plumpness had disappeared. He thought she was all eyes and cheeks and chin.

He ignored her. The loneliness of the Stretch was his and he did not want to share it with anyone else.

It was the same when he rode Jip through the areas of Cypress Hill that were not populated and where lonely country trails wove between clefts of rock and banks of heather. One such trail led upwards to Sallin's Lane and was reached by crossing a bridge further up Four-Mile River called the hill bridge.

It was November, evening time, damp, with a mist beginning to fall, when he met Ellen Pender in Sallin's Lane. He saw her riding towards him. The arrogant way she sat on her horse, as if she had been born on a saddle, annoyed him. "Snobby rich bitch," he muttered to himself. The arch of bare branches above his head added to the sense of being trapped in the narrow lane. They faced each other. She was relaxed, staring down at the damp grass, her boots resting easily against the horse's flanks. "Would you mind letting me pass first? I think the ground is firmer on your side," she said.

"It's my right to pass. I'm not moving!" Ben steadied Jip who was beginning to stretch an inquisitive nose towards the black mare. He could have moved him in towards the embankment but suddenly it seemed very important that he did not give in and make way for her horse.

"But there's a ditch on my side. I'm afraid my horse will stumble into it," she said.

"That's your problem, isn't it?" he replied.

"Oh have it your own way then!" Her face went blank, as if all the friendliness had been washed from it with a cold sponge. She stared angrily at him, then blinked.

His face seemed to trigger a memory but she still looked furious as she coaxed her horse sideways, trying to prevent the hooves slipping into the muddy hollow of the ditch. The black mare stumbled and regained her balance.

"It's all right! It's all right! I'll move," Ben panicked,

unable to bear the thought of her horse being injured, maybe even breaking a leg.

"Thank you." She had a snooty expression and her chin jutted into the air. She passed by him so close that their legs touched for an instant. Suddenly she turned towards him. "I know you! I remember now! You're…!"

He shouted "G'up" to Jip and rode away before she could finish her sentence. He found it impossible to understand his anger. Jip continued to plod along, providing no answer. But, when the sound of the black horse's hooves faded, he remembered his mother's oft-repeated belief that if any of her children cared to look truth in the face, it would tell them a few things about their behaviour. He knew then that he was jealous of Ellen Pender, jealous of her black mare that could gallop so effortlessly over the flat plains of Clemartin's Stretch, while Jip wheezed and panted like an asthmatic old smoker.

But there was something else that disturbed him and he shied away from the thought, scoffed at it, forced it from his mind, then allowed it to burn him with a sudden fierce yearning. He looked behind him. But she had disappeared through the back gate of Fairview Heights. Carefully, he guided Jip down the steep ridges of Cypress Hill and crossed the blind bridge, heading towards his home.

9

Mappo and Danny Settle a Bet

When everything changed in the new year, Danny Moone and Mappo Deane were to blame. Like Danny, Mappo had not settled into River View. At sixteen he dropped out of school and returned to Dublin city, taking up his old position outside the railway stations. At the ports he waited for the ferries to arrive but no one seemed interested in seeking his advice. Soon Mappo was forced to accept the fact that people no longer saw him as a zany young boy with a cocky grin, full of confidence and chat and useful information. He had become a young man, deep-voiced, bored and disillusioned. When travellers to the city saw him approach, they hurried past, nervously remembering advice about pickpockets and muggers. He returned to Stonyford and started searching for work in the industrial estate, in the village and on the building sites. But no one wanted a human map. The only excitement in Mappo's life was the cider gang. When winter arrived and it was too cold to gather at the bonfires, his time was spent playing cards in a flat-tyred van that had become a permanent feature in his driveway.

One night he went to Danny's house to watch a late-night film on television. After Mrs Moone and Susie went to bed, the boys shared a flagon of cider and watched an old Western, full of shoot-outs and bar-room scenes and cowboys jumping from the bedroom windows of saloons on to the backs of their horses.

"That's rubbish!" muttered Danny, glaring at the screen in disgust. "They'd break their balls if it was for real."

"Don't be such a stupid thick," yawned Mappo. "Cowboys have a way of jumping. It doesn't hurt them at all."

"Who are you calling stupid?" growled Danny. "If you know so much about it, let me see you do it."

"Oh sure. I'll just go out and saddle up my horse."

"Yeah! You just do that. Take Hackett's trusty steed. It's right next door."

"Don't be so stupid," repeated Mappo. "I'm not going near Jip. The Champs would crease me."

"Come on! Come on! Let's see you do that jump. Five pounds says you'll be singing high for the rest of your life," Danny taunted him, suddenly wide awake.

"Done!"

Without a sound, they opened the door of the stable. Mappo crouched on the roof. When Danny opened the half-door and led Jip out, Mappo yelled and jumped, missing the pony and crashing to the ground. The cider had relaxed his body and he fell like a cat. Danny gave a yell and leapt up on Jip's back. Jip reared backwards, snorting and almost throwing him, but Danny managed to cling to his mane.

Ben woke up immediately he heard Jip and stared out

the back window, trying to clear the sleep from his eyes. The scene below him looked like the high point of a nightmare.

"It's me that's supposed to be riding that stupid pony," roared Mappo, trying to pull Danny to the ground.

"Get stuffed!" Danny roared back, kicking out at Mappo with his boot.

Jip snorted again, his head rearing upwards, hemmed between the stable wall and Mrs Toner's garden wall. He lunged again when the Moones' dog began to bark. Mappo dragged Danny to the ground and, mounting Jip, managed to keep his balance by pulling hard on the horse's mane.

"There you are, stupid! I told you I could do it," yelled Mappo, all caution thrown to the wind. "Told you so, stupid!"

"Stupid! Stupid! Stupid!" His father had called him stupid that last time when Danny stood in front of the door of Wheatfield Flats and refused to let him leave. He could hear his father's voice, slurred, angry, "Get out of the way, stupid!" He could see his father's fist lashing out and his mother crying. He began to tremble. His pent-up anger exploded.

"Shut up! Shut the fuck up!" he yelled at Mappo, picking up a stone.

Ben was running down the stairs as if there were flames licking his heels. By the time he reached the back door, Danny had flung the stone. Mappo was still trying to control the trembling pony. The stone sailed over his head. It crashed through Mrs Toner's back patio door, shattering the glass.

Lights snapped on along the row of houses. Faces appeared at bedroom windows. Ben was just in time to catch a glimpse of Danny and Mappo, climbing like slithery eels back into Moones' garden. He could see Mrs Moone, her face creased with worry, slapping at Danny's head as he dashed past her in through the kitchen doorway.

On the other side, Mrs Toner was torn between fury over her broken patio glass and delight that Jip had finally disturbed the peace. "I knew this would happen!" she screamed at the Hackett family, who had tumbled from their beds when they heard the commotion. "You're responsible for this!" Her finger shook as she pointed it towards Ben. "I saw you fling that stone. You deliberately vandalised my house. The police are on their way to arrest you."

A siren and flashing blue light added to the confusion. A young guard opened his notebook and began to take details of the damage. He eyed Jip uneasily, standing well back from the pony's nervous hooves. When Ben made noises, deep in his throat, it seemed to soothe the horse, even though Mrs Toner and Mrs Hackett were trying to outshout each other.

"I demand my rights as a citizen. Impound this animal!" shrieked Mrs Toner.

"I demand my rights as a citizen. Impound this woman!" shrieked Mrs Hackett.

The other guard was an older man, known as Fire Fighter because of his habit of dousing the flames of the wasteland bonfires with flagons of cider whenever he caught the cider gang drinking.

He watched Ben settling Jip into his stable. Mrs

Hackett apologised to Mrs Toner in a voice that seemed to strangle her and promised to pay the costs of repairing her patio door. Ben offered to sweep up the broken glass. "No thanks," sniffed Mrs Toner. "I don't want the smell of horse manure in my home."

"We have to talk, kid," said Fire Fighter, leading the way into the kitchen.

Mrs Hackett made tea for everyone while Ben tried to explain what had happened. "I know I was the first person she saw when she looked out her window. But that's because I ran out to Jip. The window was broken by then. I didn't throw that stone."

"Would you like to tell me who did throw it?" asked Fire Fighter.

"It wasn't my Ben," said Mrs Hackett, firmly, when her son refused to answer. "He's more to do with his time than throw stones at that Snob Blob next door."

"That's as may be," said the guard, taking a cup of tea from her. "I have my suspicions as to who might be responsible. But I can't prove anything, no more than you can prove that it wasn't your son. And he's going to have to get rid of that horse."

Ben felt as if someone had punched him hard in the centre of his stomach. "You can't take Jip away. You can't!"

"Take it easy, kid," said Fire Fighter. "I'm not taking the horse from you. I'm only saying that you'll have to move him somewhere else. Mrs Toner will be within her rights to insist on that."

"Could I leave him on the wastelands?"

"Sorry. That's council land and they would impound him. And I suspect that Mrs Toner will make sure they

do. The pound will be here tomorrow. I suggest you have
the animal stabled somewhere else by then."

10

Working for Main Man

Ben took a deep breath and knocked on Main Man's cottage door. All night he had tossed and turned, Fire Fighter's warning haunting his dreams. When morning came, his thoughts had turned full circle to the stables on Highfern Row.

"You needn't think that I'm taking back that animal!" Main Man stood in front of his doorway. A filthy T-shirt strained across his chest. His stomach bulged over his trousers. Ben thought of Danny's nickname for the fat man, then banished it instantly in case Main Man could read his mind. Three months previously Danny had swaggered past the dealer on the wastelands, shouting, "Blubber Belly McMullen." Before he could draw breath, Main Man spun him around and traced the tip of a knife along his jawbone. "What did you call me, pup?" he demanded.

"M...Mr McMu...Mul...len."

"Say it again, pup!" ordered Main Man. "Let me hear it. Sing it out loud so that nobody gets confused ever again." A thin trickle of blood ran down the side of Danny's throat. The cut was only a pin-prick. But his face was the colour of a plucked and frozen chicken when, hoarse from shouting "Mr Main Man McMullen," he staggered away from the threatening knife.

"You bought that pony from me at Downshandon Market and I don't take returns from pups who change their mind." The dealer smacked his fist against the palm of his hand.

"I don't want to return Jip. I want somewhere safe to keep him at night, or else he'll be sent to the horse pound," Ben replied.

"So they threw him out of River View. Well well well! What a surprise! And you expect me to give you free board and lodgings for that hack. Have a bit of sense, pup, and sell him to Canine Chops." He scratched his chest and prepared to close the door in Ben's face.

"Wait!" Ben pushed against it. "I don't expect any favours from you. I'll give you my labour for free if I can leave Jip here. I'll clean out the place and look after the horses at night. They're still breaking out and you'll be in real trouble if people keep complaining and the pound comes around."

"This is private land. I can keep whatever I like on it and it's nobody's business but mine." But Ben noticed the way Main Man's eye slitted and guessed that the dealer had been warned already. This gave him the courage to outstare him.

"I'll make sure that the horses don't escape when you're down in the Stony Arms at night and..."

"You're a cute little pup, right enough," interrupted the dealer. The black band holding his eye-patch in place was stark against his angry face.

But Ben could see that he was weakening. He kept his

voice steady. "At least I'll make it a more comfortable place for the horses." From the back garden he heard a low-pitched sound as a horse sensed Jip's presence and greeted him.

Jip did not reply. His ears had flopped in dismay when Ben had reached the cottage.

"When's the pound coming round to collect him?" asked Main Man.

"This afternoon."

"They're getting very officious, snooping and prying and asking questions. They wouldn't know what hard work was, even if it bit them on their lily-white hands." Main Man spat out the words. "OK, pup. If you do all them things you say you're going to do, we might be able to come to some arrangement. I'll give you two weeks' work and if you don't prove your worth in that time, you won't see your pony's hooves for dust. Understand?"

Mrs Hackett was furious when he told her about his new job.

"You mean you're giving up your job in Campion's?"

"I have to. I won't be able to go to Main Man's if I have to stack shelves as well." The dealer had agreed to feed Jip as part of the deal so Ben no longer needed to earn money for his food.

Mrs Hackett fretted and scolded. "I never heard so much rubbish in all my life. You'd be far better off selling the pony and getting your money back on him. I don't like you working for that fellow. Anyone who looks as shifty as he does can't be up to any good."

Danny told him that he was off his head. Jip wasn't worth the labour Main Man would wring out of him. No one was going to get rich from the sweat of Danny's brow. Ben ignored him. Since the night Danny had destroyed his dream, he no longer had any feelings left for his one-time friend.

On Highfern Row, he did two hours' work before going to school and returned as soon as classes ended in the afternoon. Main Man was a demanding taskmaster. But Ben was young and strong. Most important, he was close to Jip. In the beginning he had been disgusted that his pony had to return to the flies and the dirt and the smell. But as the months passed, he began to make changes. Each cottage had four rooms and, except for one cottage that remained locked at all times, the horses sometimes used them as a shelter at night. Down came the broken doors between the rooms. The wood was rotten and the hinges broke away easily. Mappo and Danny came by with wheelbarrows and took them for their bonfires. After Ben finished hosing down the cottages, he found some tins of whitewash and painted the walls. The Charney Champs offered to help.

Main Man watched the invasion of the girls without expression, then disappeared. He was spending a lot of time at race meetings and Ben soon learned to recognise the signs of a bad day's gambling, followed by a visit to drown his sorrows in the Stony Arms. His face would darken and swell with temper, his fists swinging at anything within reach.

There was a lot of bluster and bluff about Main Man that Ben soon learned to ignore. But he learned first to dodge the dealer's fists. At night the horses no longer escaped. It was often midnight before Main Man returned home. Ben would hear him stumbling along the river path, singing at the top of his voice. He would fall into bed and sleep immediately, his eye-patch slipping sideways, and Ben would quickly turn away from the puckered skin, terrified in case he would find himself looking into a vacant hole in his face.

A summer morning on Clemartin's Stretch was the most glorious time of the day. He would bring the horses to the grassy flatland and let them run free, their hooves drumming the damp grass, his eyes scanning the horizon, hoping to catch a glimpse of Ellen Pender. When they met they ignored each other, making a great show of galloping close so that each could stare coldly at the sky above the other's shoulders. The only other person he ever saw was the old woman, Cathy Dill. Like Craigy, with his wind-burned face and peaked cap, Cathy Dill was a startling contrast to the "blow-ins" from River View. Her bushy grey hair flowed down her back and she wore a long skirt. Ben used to see her in Campion's Supermarket, filling her trolley with cat food. These old people, once such a vital part of the rural village, looked like relics of the past among the brightly dressed, noisy population that was changing the face of Stonyford.

Her cats stretched languidly on the walls of the blind bridge, watching Ben from their hazy green eyes. She would come to her door and wave to him, then whistle softly through her teeth. The cats would stretch, arch their backs and leap from the walls, hurrying towards their morning feed.

In school, Ben found it impossible to concentrate. Before the start of the summer holidays, Mrs Hackett was summoned to the school for a talk with Mr Oakes, Ben's form tutor. For a week afterwards he had to listen to his mother repeating every word that Mr Oakes had uttered.

Eventually, she got tired repeating the form tutor's caustic comments and began to insist that if, as Mr Oakes insisted, Ben Hackett was a boil on the skin of academia (at this stage Mrs Hackett's voice always rose in a shrill parody of the form tutor's disapproving tone), then he should leave school and make space for those who were interested in learning, and did not sit all day gazing out of windows or talk in their sleep during maths.

Mr Hackett said that Ben should try and get a job in the electronics factory where he worked. He brought home an application form and, despite his son's loud protests, insisted on Ben filling it out. The thought of working on an assembly line filled him with dread. But his summer report was a bomb, ready to explode. He had walked out of two examinations and bluffed his way through the remainder.

"Under existing circumstances, Ben Hackett is a waste of space in my class!" was the statement that Mr Oakes penned on the bottom of the report.

"D-minus!" Mrs Hackett groaned with disbelief, hitting her son on his shoulders with the report sheet until it was reduced to flitters. "D-minus!" she repeated, unable to believe it. "And that's in your strong subjects! That's the end of your little picnic on Highfern Row. I want you out of there, pronto! Get down to the industrial estate and find a job!"

Ben decided that it would be wise not to argue with his mother. He made his way to Highfern Row, sick with apprehension in case he would not be allowed to keep Jip in the stables.

Main Man's hair had grown long. It was greasy, tied back with a piece of string. He scratched his chin when

Ben told him the news. "Well well well, we can't have that now, can we? Those factories would bend a man's brain in half. Not that you're worth a penny of the sixty pounds a week I'll pay you, but if you want a full-time job running this place for me, you can have it. I've enough things on my plate at the moment."

Mrs Hackett was less than pleased when Ben told her about Main Man's offer but her anger was muted by the fact that her husband had enquired and discovered that there were no longer any jobs available in the electronics factory.

Ben had no regrets about leaving school. Even though he hated working for Main Man, everything he wanted to know about life was contained on Highfern Row. To Main Man, horses were just beasts to be bartered and passed around for a price. He never saw their courage, their patience, their affection. So what if Ben Hackett got D-minus in his report? That was not important to the horses. All they asked was that he love them and care for them. But even without those simple things, they were willing to work until their hearts wore out. Ben had found out about Jip's past. For years he had stood on the pier at a seaside resort, a tourist attraction in the sun, wearing a top hat and a dicky-bow around his neck, while children clambered on his back to have their photographs taken. Day after day, swatting flies with his tail, watching the world walking past, he stood still, enduring, uncomplaining. So when his mother went on about him being an odd-bod and preferring animals to human beings, Ben couldn't figure why she was getting so steamed up.

At the end of the week, Main Man gave him his first

week's wages, minus thirty pounds for Jip's board and food. Ben moaned at what was left. "Just remember this, pup, it would cost you over seventy pounds a week to keep that hack in the pound," snapped Main Man. Ben moaned even louder when Mrs Hackett demanded twenty pounds for her son's board and food.

"It's not fair. That's all I've left!" He looked down in dismay at the ten-pound note in his hand.

"Fair or not, I'm taking my share," replied his mother, unmoved. "I may be just the skivvy...the invisible skivvy—" she paused dramatically "—who has to cook your dinners and then throw them into the bin because her waste-of-space-son can't be bothered coming home in time to eat them. But that doesn't mean I'm not entitled to a fair salary."

In her yellow tracksuit with its turquoise strips, she reminded him of a shrill little canary. But when Ben looked at her worried face, he knew that her scolding was just a shield to hide her anxiety. She was light when he lifted her up in his arms and carried her around the kitchen. "I'll be famous some day, Ma. I'll have more horses than you'll know how to count and I'll shower you with so much money, you'll have to climb a ladder to see over the top of it."

"And pigs will sing opera on the eighth day of the week!" she insisted, smiling at last. "You always make me laugh, Ben. But that doesn't solve the problems. You only had another year to go before doing your Leaving Cert. What are you going to do with the rest of your life if you haven't got a proper education? And I certainly don't like you working for that slick-fisted crook, McMullen. I'm afraid for you. Sell Jip and get out of that place."

"I can't Ma. I can't leave Jip. I won't!"

"Oh, you and your daft loving," she sighed and smacked him gently on his face. Then she brushed back his thatch of straw-blond hair, kissed him on his forehead and said no more.

11

Ben's Visit to Fairview Heights

One morning Main Man attached a horse-box to his van. "I'm collecting a horse for the Barclaid brat. Another birthday present." He snorted, scornfully. "As if that poser kid would be able to tell the difference between a horse and a rhinoceros."

He returned that evening with a chestnut, a sprightly long-legged gelding. "Take him away, pup, and give him the beauty treatment. He's going to be stabled in Fairview Heights."

When Ben finished grooming the chestnut, Main Man inspected the sleek coat and plaited mane. He nodded, satisfied. "You'd better come with me. The van has been giving a bit of trouble and I'll need you to go for help if it breaks down."

The van rattled along the river road, pulling the horse-box. Olive Bricken cycled over the humped bridge and almost crashed into the side of it. Main Man beeped angrily and Olive nearly fell off her bicycle when she saw his angry face glaring at her from the window. The van continued through Stonyford Village, moaning like a cat in pain when it began the climb towards Cypress Hill.

A park had been made on the hill with paved paths, wooden benches and picnic tables. In the evening, young people rode their ponies through the leafy avenue of trees. Ben never noticed Ellen Pender among them. She seemed to prefer the early-morning loneliness of Clemartin's Stretch.

Flat-roofed, wooden stables had been built at the back of Fairview Heights with a row of horse shoes over the doors.

"They're not a patch on Jip's stable," Ben thought. It was eight months since Jip's departure from River View. His twin brothers used the stable for their racing pigeons.

The van belched black smoke from its exhaust. When it shuddered to a halt, the jolt made the front windows fall down.

"Unload the horse, pup," ordered Main Man. "I want to have a quick word in Davy Pender's ear about a certain land deal."

There was no sign of the groom whom Ben had met on his previous visit. He prepared to unload the horse.

"Is that Douglas's horse?" Ellen had emerged from one of the stables carrying a bale of hay. She put it down and leaned against the wall of the stable, arms folded and a wary glint in her eyes.

"Yes," he replied, fumbling at the bolt on the horse-box. She always made him feel so clumsy.

"Douglas! Douglas! It's arrived!" She cupped her hands to her mouth and shouted in the direction of her house. When there was no reply, she shook her head, impatiently.

"That's just typical of Douglas. Imagine!" There was mud on her jeans and stalks of hay on her navy sweater. "He's getting a horse for his birthday and he doesn't want to know. I'll never forget how excited I was when I got Dark Sprite."

"So you should be—for £3,000!" Ben thought. The memory roughened his voice. "Just move aside, please, while I unload the horse. Don't crowd him. He scares easily." He dropped the ramp. Together they inspected the chestnut.

"Oh, you beauty, you beauty. Let me have a look at him." While she spoke, Ellen was running her hands over the animal in an expert way that reminded Ben of the blacksmith, Craigy.

"He's a good one. Main Man knows his stuff when it comes to picking horses."

A cat scurried from the stable, jumping on to the ramp with a loud mew. Hooves drummed against the paved slabs as the horse did a scampering dance. He appeared to be petrified of his new surroundings, rearing backwards when Ellen tried to handle him. As soon as Ben spoke softly into his ear, blowing into his nostrils, the horse calmed down.

"How did you do that?" She sounded curious.

"It's nothing, just words."

"But the horse seemed to understand you."

"Of course. I speak his language."

"Go on," she ordered. "Do it again."

"Ah, it's nothing." He felt stupid. "I was only messing."

"No, you weren't. Go on, show me." He wondered if she were teasing him, but there was only interest in her face.

"All right. First you've got to stand beside the animal, really close, like this."

Without her riding cap, her hair fell around her face,

black and straight, touching her shoulders. He could smell the fresh, apple scent of shampoo. She moved her lips close to the horse's ear, trying to repeat the strange guttural sounds Ben uttered.

"It just sounds like gibberish!" She moved away, as if something scared her.

"That's what my mother says." Ben shrugged. The moment was broken. "Maybe you're both right. It doesn't really matter as long as the animal understands."

"You have a strange way with horses." She sounded envious. "I don't understand it. When I ride past Highfern Row and see you working with them, I envy you. I'll never know my horse the way you seem to know your horses." She hesitated, looked hard at him and muttered, "It's a pity you don't know how to treat people as well as you treat animals."

"What's that supposed to mean?"

She grimaced."You know what I mean. That time on Sallin's Lane. You were so rude. Like some big macho man strutting past on your big pony, blocking up the lane as if it was your right of way and nobody else's. You're the same on the Stretch, full of airs and graces. It's common land, you know. It belongs to everyone, and that includes me!"

He stepped back, lifting his arms in front of his face and warding off her anger in mock-dismay. Ellen Pender was obviously someone who did not mince her words.

It amazed him that she thought he was the one who was showing off and he wondered how she would react if he told her that he felt like choking with envy every time he saw her on her black horse. But the words were mixed up inside his head and he knew he'd only muddle them up even more if he tried to explain. He began to laugh.

"What's so funny?" Her chin lifted.

"I'm sorry." He could see that she was embarrassed by his laughter. "I can't understand why you should think that. Jip is not exactly the kind of pony that gives anyone airs and graces."

"He wouldn't win any beauty contests if that's what you mean." She chuckled. "But he's got such a faithful old face. I just know he'd carry you through fire and water if you asked him to." She had summed up Jip's character in a few words and, for the first time since Ben met her in the grounds of Charney House, he began to like her again.

As if reading his thoughts, she pointed towards the chestnut tree. "Do you remember that evening when we met and this place was just an old dump? That's the tree we climbed."

The memory of that night, and of her closeness when they sat together on the branch listening to the muffled autumn sounds, came back to him. He wondered what it would feel like if she moved so close to him again. But Ellen Pender was no longer a child and the thought was a hot flash of pleasure that came so suddenly and unexpectedly that he had to turn his back on her.

"Am I interrupting something important—or can anyone join in?" drawled a voice.

The youth who stood watching Ellen had a pouting lip and a long face. His hair swept back from his high forehead. For an instant, Ben recoiled, as if the person standing before him was a familiar but unpleasant sight. Then he realised that he had only seen the youth once before, on the day of Ellen's fourteenth birthday. Yet his dislike of him was as instantaneous as it had been on that sunny day when he had watched the two families from the shelter of the rhododendrons.

"Douglas Barclaid! Where were you? I've been calling you for ages," Ellen demanded.

Douglas ignored her. He inspected the chestnut without much interest. "Is this the famous birthday present?"

"Yes. Isn't he fabulous?" she insisted.

Douglas shrugged. "He's not exactly the kind of horse power I like, as you should know." He raised his eyebrows suggestively at her. "Do you fancy a ride?" When she blushed and frowned, he said: "Horse riding, dear child. What else do you think I meant? You take your nag and I'll put this fellow through his paces. See what he's made of."

"Give him time to settle," Ben advised. "He's travelled a lot and he's nervous."

"Who is this guy?" Douglas looked at Ben as if he had just noticed him for the first time.

"He's Ben Hackett," said Ellen. "Don't you remember? I told you about him. He's always on the Stretch with the horses."

"Oh, yes." Douglas smiled. "You work in that knacker's yard on Highfern Row."

Ben did not move or look away from him. Their mutual dislike was almost tangible.

"I help Main Man to look after his horses, if that's what you mean. I've done a lot of work on the Row and I don't like it being called a knacker's yard."

Douglas turned to Ellen. "Oh dear, it seems I've

offended Hackett and his hacks." He had a baying laugh that set Ben's teeth on edge.

"Very funny," she snapped. "But he knows a lot more than either of us about horses. I'd listen to him if I were you."

"Well, you're not me. So shut up, Ellen!" Douglas went into a tack-room at the side of the stable and emerged carrying a saddle and bridle. The horse trembled and took a step backwards when the saddle was slapped across his back. Douglas worked quickly, fastening the girth straps. He made no effort to check them for comfort. It was the same with the bridle. The browband was fastened so tightly that Ben sensed the horse's discomfort, while the bit was too high and stretched his mouth.

"You're hurting him!" he snapped. "It's far too tight."

Douglas turned around. "Could I remind you that you are the delivery boy and I am the owner of this horse. So back off and mind your own business."

"This *is* my business. You should loosen that bit. It's pulling his mouth and it'll make him bleed."

Douglas tilted back his head and sniffed the air, wrinkling his nose in disgust. "That's the worst of working in a knacker's yard. You get to smell of horse-shit after a while."

"Stop it, Douglas!" Ellen was standing between the two of them. "Why do you always have to be such a pain?"

"If you get up on that horse you're dead meat," Ben said, feeling his anger churning sharp and quivering inside him.

"Repeat that again, dick-head," said Douglas, moving away from the horse and sauntering towards Ben. He was still smiling when he pushed Ellen aside. He was tall and well-built. Years of rugby training had added strength to his shoulders. But Ben had spent a lot of time mucking out stables, exercising horses and ducking Main Man's fists. He moved quickly aside, lashed out with his fist and slammed it into Douglas's shoulder. Douglas lashed out and Ben went staggering backwards, the stables spinning around him.

"Stop it…stop it!" Ellen kept shouting.

They ignored her. All Ben could hear was his own breath, a gasp of triumph when he hit Douglas again and the heavier boy fell to the ground. His nose began to bleed. When his hand touched his face, he stared in disbelief at the blood. At his head, the chestnut's hooves fidgeted nervously.

"Stop that! This instant!" Another voice echoed Ellen's command. Ben froze at the sight of Mr Pender. "You hooligan! I saw what you did. How would you like a charge of assault brought against you?" He helped Douglas to his feet. "You'd better go inside, Douglas, and get that wound dressed immediately."

"It wasn't Ben's fault," cried Ellen. "Douglas was to blame."

"Really, Ellen! You saw your best friend kicked to the ground by a guttersnipe and you dare to contradict me. I'm quite amazed at your attitude."

"It's from riding out on the Stretch with him," shouted Douglas, his face white with fury. "She meets up with him every morning."

"Is this true, Ellen?" asked Mr Pender, quietly.

"No, it's not." She held her hands stiffly against her sides and returned her father's gaze. "But even if it was—what of it?"

Mr Pender turned to Ben. His eyes glazed over as if he was addressing something invisible. "I don't want scum like you hanging around my daughter. Keep to your own side of the river in future or you'll feel more than the weight of my words. If I catch you anywhere near Cypress Hill again, I'll have you charged with trespassing and assault. Is that understood?"

Douglas smirked, then quickly dabbed a handkerchief to his nose. Ellen looked as if she was about to burst into tears. But instead her chin jutted forward. "You can't stop him coming up Cypress Hill if he wants to."

Mr Pender glared. "Kindly hold your tongue and go inside, Ellen."

"It's not fair. Ben hit Douglas only because he wouldn't stop hurting his horse. He should be reported to the Society for the Prevention of Cruelty to Animals. Look at the way he put the bit into his horse's mouth."

"I'm warning you, Ellen. Stop carrying on like that. I'm appalled at the change in you recently."

"How can you see a change in me. You're never here! Never! Never!" Suddenly she was shrieking at her father. "And now you're going off again and you just want to get rid of me by packing me..."

"Your mother is waiting for you." Ben shivered at the tone of her father's voice. Ellen instantly stopped shouting. Her black hair swung around her face when she bent her head. She began to cry, silently. "I'll have something to say to her about your behaviour. Now get this yob off my property, immediately, McMullen."

Ben had not noticed the horse-dealer in the background. Main Man reached out and cuffed him across the back of his head.

"Right you are, sir." The horse-dealer licked his lips. "Oh, by the way, Mr Pender. Have you made your decision about my piece of land on Highfern Row yet?"

"When I do, McMullen, you'll be the first to know about it. As I've told you before, it will not be for some months yet, perhaps even a year. Now, please leave my property."

"That's fine, Mr Pender. I just thought I'd ask. No harm in asking I always say. Good day to you, sir. Come on, pup. You've outworn your welcome. Do what the gentleman says. Get moving."

12

Strange Happenings on Highfern Row

On the anniversary of Ben's first year in Highfern Row, Clemartin's Stretch was a white blanket. When the snow melted the horses pawed the soft earth and dug deep, their strong teeth pulling up roots and chomping them into pulp. As soon as spring came, Ben brought the horses to the Stretch and waited for Ellen Pender to appear. Daffodils and primroses blazed for a brief, dizzy period and faded away. Still there was no sign of her. One morning he saw her horse in the distance. He dismounted from Jip and waited for her to draw nearer, swinging from elation to anger and back again within the few minutes it took Dark Sprite to reach him.

He remembered the last time they met, the look of contempt on her father's face, a look that reduced Ben into something not worth noticing. Main Man's van had belched black smoke, rattled and snorted away from Fairview Heights and Ben, staring straight ahead, had allowed his anger to include everyone who had witnessed the scene at the stables. He told himself that he never wanted to see Ellen Pender again. Yet, waiting for her to pass along the river road or scanning the horizon on the

Stretch had become an established part of his day and he could not break the habit, no matter how much he argued with himself. Dark Sprite drew nearer. He bit back his disappointment when he realised it was Robert, the Penders' groom, who was riding her.

"Hi Ben! How's Main Man?" The little man was in a mood for talking. He told Ben that his boss was working in Spain on a major Pender Development contract.

"He's away a lot of the time now. The missus usually travels with him. She likes the high-flying life and the chance of a winter tan. That's the way to live. Plenty of old dosh and all the time in the world to spend it." He sucked in his lips over the word "dosh" as if savouring a most succulent flavour.

"How about his daughter, what's her name...?" Ben asked casually.

"Ellen. She's away at boarding school for the year. Her father decided that he didn't want her running wild when him and the missus were travelling so much." The groom chuckled. "She's a right little fire-cracker. The trouble there was about that school. Mind you, she didn't pick that stubborn streak off the trees. Like father, like daughter. Those two were shaped from the same mould, right enough."

There was relief in riding the Stretch and knowing that Ellen would not appear. Only then did Ben realise how much time he had spent watching and waiting and thinking about her.

His loathing for his job grew deeper with each passing month. It was not the work itself that disturbed him. The cottages had been transformed into comfortable stables. He had cordoned off parts of the gardens so that the land had a chance to recover from the horse's constant grazing. Shoots of new grass were thick and green. Soon the horses would be able to graze on the fresh pastures and he would replant the area they had left.

Some of the ponies looked thin and worn-out when they arrived at Highfern Row. They were grazed on Clemartin's Stretch and when they looked fat and healthy, were moved on, to be sold abroad or in other parts of the country. Parents who had little knowledge of horses were easily deceived by healthy coats and their reasonable selling price. They bought them for a son or daughter who wanted riding lessons. When the children began to make demands on the animals, it would then be discovered that their spirits had been broken forever. Those ponies were never traced back to Highfern Row.

Ben tried not to think of the fate of the horses who were examined by Taggy Somers and driven off in the direction of Canine Chops.

Main Man seemed satisfied with Ben, willing to allow him a free hand in looking after the stables. Whenever the dealer was off visiting a race meeting or a horse fair, Craigy would call and inspect the animals or Ben would bring them to his forge.

"You watch that Main Man!" Craigy warned him. "His gambling mania's getting worse. He's in poor shape." The blacksmith inspected a pony's eyes. "He's still borrowing money from Murty Slomes. Davy Pender's next big job will be developing the Stretch and Main Man thinks he's going to make a fortune on this bit of land leading into it. So he's spending money as if there was no tomorrow. Just watch him and don't trust him an inch."

As time went on, and the dealer's trust in Ben continued to grow, the boy could no longer turn a blind eye to his activities. He was finding out secrets that made him shiver. He wondered what Craigy would say if he told him about the jeep driven by a man called Dessie Horgan that sometimes arrived late at night to Highfern Row with a horse-box attached. On such nights, Main Man did not visit the Stony Arms but worked swiftly and silently with Dessie to unload heavy containers from the back of the horse-box.

"Have you got a pair of wooden legs or something?" he hissed at Ben, the first time the boy had witnessed a delivery. "Get busy and lend some muscle over here."

The locked cottage was opened and the containers left inside. Main Man became even snappier than usual while the containers remained hidden. A few nights later, another jeep and horse-box would arrive. This time there would be a different driver, Eddie Lowe. Just as silently, the containers were removed. As soon as the tail-lights of the horse-box disappeared over the summit of the blind bridge, the atmosphere on Highfern Row lifted and the tension left Main Man's face.

"It's a small storage service I offer my friends," he explained, when Ben asked about the horse-box. "I haven't done it for a while but I need money fast. If I hear you spreading stories about this around River View you can say goodbye to chewing meat for the rest of your life. And they'll be making burgers out of that hack of yours over in Canine Chops before you can say 'pass the ketchup.' Understand what I'm saying, pup?"

With his feet dangling above ground level and his anorak tightening like a noose around his neck, Ben did not feel like arguing. He was in deep trouble and there was an uneasy suspicion at the back of his mind that it was going to become a lot worse.

The dealer was gambling, spending a lot of time at Fortune's, a new betting shop that had opened in Stonyford Village. He would drive off to a race meeting in his van, promising to return that night. Sometimes he did not appear again for two or three days, and when he did come home his clothes were dusty, his face bloated with self-pity, his humour atrocious.

When Main Man went to the races, Ben stayed overnight, wrapping himself in a sleeping bag and dozing on an old sofa that sagged in the middle. The sounds of Highfern Row kept waking him, the constant mewing of Cathy Dill's cats, the restless pacing of horses. Sometimes the biker passed by the window, speeding along the river road towards Clemartin's Stretch or heading towards River View to scorch the surface of the blind bridge and tour the wastelands.

"He's a speed-freak," said Danny, when Ben asked him if he ever saw him. "I'd love to smash his face in. But he's fast. Fast." Danny shook his head, a note of reluctant admiration in his voice.

One night the biker killed a cat that ran under the wheels of his bike. When Ben went outside, Cathy Dill was sobbing. She lifted the body of the cat from the river road.

"Poor poor Charlie," she kept repeating. Ben helped her to bury Charlie. In the distance, they heard the revving engine of the motorbike.

Murty Slomes, the moneylender, arrived one morning and announced himself by kicking open the kitchen door of Main Man's cottage. His wide shoulders filled the entrance and, for the first time, Ben saw Main Man shrink back in fear. They argued loudly. Murty blustered and demanded payments on debts that he was owed. His bullish face reddened with temper when Main Man wheedled, made excuses and handed over a sum of money that did little to pacify Murty.

"I'll be back, McMullen. I'll be back! Only that I know you're shifting this land, I'd have had my men spreadeagle you on the wastelands long ago."

"Bloody moneylenders, they're all the same. They'd take the last penny from your pocket and leave you belly-up in the gutter," Main Man muttered after Murty left.

Mr Hackett often made the same comment. "Murty Slomes is a bloodsucker, the poor man's bank. He's a leech who lives off the misfortune of others." There were few people on River View who disagreed with him. Ben shivered and wondered how much longer he could cope with the suffocating atmosphere on Highfern Row.

13

Mappo's Discovery

A week after Murty's visit, Ben was digging ragwort when Mappo called over to Highfern Row.

"Hey, Ben, is Main Man around?" he enquired casually. He relaxed when he heard that the dealer had gone to Stonyford Village to place a bet in Fortune's. "How's it going then?" He circled the horses, eyeing them nervously.

"So so. Why?"

"You'd be well advised to get out of this kip. I've heard that Main Man's shifting stuff through the cottages. It's only a matter of time before the police get wind of it."

"I don't know what you're talking about."

"Oh sure! Listen. It's no skin off my nose what he does. But Blubber-Belly," Mappo instinctively glanced over his shoulder, "will be in big trouble and you'll be there along with him as a receiver of stolen goods."

"How do you know that?"

"I know a man. His word's good." Mappo tapped his nose in a "don't be so nosy" gesture and smiled, ambiguously. "I'm warning you for your own good."

"It's a pity you didn't think about 'my own good'

before you and Moone let my pony loose that night."

"Yeah…well! Sorry about that. That's water under the blind bridge, as they say. Come on. Leave the animals for a bit. I want to show you something."

Ben wanted to say no but, responding to some inner excitement that Mappo could not quite manage to hide, he followed him over the blind bridge, hurrying to keep pace with the older boy's quickening stride. They came to the end of the wastelands where a large rubbish dump sprawled in a bed of black refuse sacks and rusting cans. Once past this eyesore, they reached a quiet country lane that was seldom used by anyone. Thick leafy ferns and nettles grew beneath the hedgerows.

"There's an entrance somewhere around here," said Mappo, pointing to a dense clump of greenery.

"Where?"

"Through those bushes. There's some kind of a field and there should be the remains of a cottage on it. I figured it out from an old map of Stonyford."

Ben knew better than to doubt Mappo's word. "So what's that got to do with me?"

"Don't be so thick. You're looking for somewhere safe to keep your horse. You can't use the wastelands in case he's impounded. But if we can get through those bushes this could be the very place. There's a stream running through it that's probably a tributary of Four-Mile River. Look, I've worked it all out."

From the pocket of his jeans he pulled out a piece of paper on which he had pencilled a rough drawing of what the land would look like if it was cleared. Mappo traced his finger over the curved lines and Ben could almost see the gap in the clumpy bushes and beyond, to where a trail had been obliterated but might, just might, lead to a haven for Jip.

"I did a bit of snooping around and found out that the field belongs to a fellow called Dempsey who's now living in Birmingham." Mappo peered into a cluster of ferns. "He's just letting the land lie because he reckons it'll be developed for building sooner or later. I've been in touch with him. He says it's OK to keep the horse there if I can get through to the field."

"That was a lot of trouble, Mappo," Ben sounded surprised.

Mappo casually waved away his thanks. "I always felt bad about the old pony having to go back to that dump."

Suddenly it was possible to hope. To imagine taking Jip from Highfern Row, to a place where he could shelter from the wind against a line of trees and rest his old bones on the soft earth. But the gorse bushes, beginning to bud with early summer blossom, the overhanging hawthorn trees and the briars formed an impenetrable barrier. It was an impossible dream. When Ben left Mappo and returned to Highfern Row, the tall, lanky youth with the ponytail and stooped shoulders was still walking up and down in front of this wilderness. For the first time since he moved to River View, the old challenge was back in Mappo's eyes. He had prowled the city and discovered her secret places. Now he was going to try and uncover the secrets lying beyond the wild gorse.

Another week passed and Ben had almost forgotten about Mappo's idea. Then Danny called to Highfern Row one afternoon. It was his half-day from school and he wore his school uniform jumper over a pair of jeans. Mrs Moone had refused to allow him to drop out of school and he would be sitting his Leaving Certificate examination in a few weeks. But Ben knew that he regularly missed classes and instead took a bus to the city centre. Mrs Hackett had seen him once in Henry Street. He was playing his mouth-organ but disappeared into the crowd when she called his name.

"Come on," he nodded brusquely at Ben. "Mappo wants a word."

They hardly spoke on the way to the country lane. When Ben looked closely, he saw that feathery sprays of Lady's Lace and ferns had been cleared to form a narrow opening. "Are you coming through?" he asked Danny.

"You must be joking. Don't you know I'm allergic to country air. You're on your own, Hackett." He nodded abruptly then hurried away, leaving Ben to force his way through a trail, where nettles and briars had not quite managed to hide a path that had been carved into the ground over centuries by countless footprints. Ben was soon covered in nettle stings and insect bites. Midges swarmed over his head and made his scalp itchy. But it was worth every difficult step.

Mappo was standing in the centre of a small clearing, slashing at knee-high grass and weeds with a machete. The ruins of the old cottage were still standing, although the roof had caved in. Ivy spread over the walls and, in the crevices of the stonework, tiny puffs of white weed pushed their way towards the light. There was even a rusty gate with creepers twined around the bars. Scutch grass grew in wild clumps and a carpet of wood garlic released a pungent scent under his feet.

Gorse was the enemy. It had invaded the land, a prickly, formidable foe with stout limbs and a dazzling yellow face. But the land could be cleared. Ben kept repeating this wonderful idea to himself. It would take months of work, uprooting weeds, slashing briars and thistles. He could hear the sound of water, and Mappo, with his unerring sense of direction, beckoned him to follow. They stopped beside a stream.

"So! What do you think?" Mappo tried to look uninterested but he had a grin on his face and Ben figured it had to be the size of the sun.

"You still haven't lost it, Mappo. You're a genius." Ben grabbed him by the shoulders and the boys, in a burst of excitement, flung themselves down on the rough grass, wrestling and laughing and thumping each other until they were breathless.

"Don't forget Danny Moone," Mappo gasped. "Most evenings he came and helped clear this lot and it's bloody hard work, I'll tell you that for nothing."

Mappo lay on his stomach, running blades of grass through his fingers. The rasping surface of the grass cut his skin but he did not seem to notice. "I hate River View," he spoke angrily. "All those rows of grey houses and those wastelands. They give me the creeps."

"You don't have to stay on the wastelands."

"So what am I supposed to do? Keep trudging around the industrial estate, looking for work day after day. Those guys down there don't even see me any more. I'm just a form-filler, someone to be filed away and forgotten. They call us the river rats. Did you know that? Rats! Just because we keep returning to the same place all the time. Remember that rat you had when you were a kid, what did you call her...Sheba or something daft like that? Nobody wanted her either." He began to laugh. It was the unfunniest sound Ben had ever heard. "But we're not rats. Rats have some order in their lives. They have a purpose. What's my purpose, Ben? What the hell am I doing in this village on the way to nowhere?"

Ben did not know what to say. But Mappo wasn't looking for answers. His mind was made up. He stood up and waved his hand around the wilderness. "This is all I ever want to discover about Stonyford. It's a sort of parting gift to you—to make up for Jip and all that messing. You can do what you like with it. And I won't mention it to anyone. Nor will Danny. Are we quits now?"

"We're quits. And thanks, Mappo."

A week later Mappo left Stonyford. He went without saying goodbye to anyone. When Ben returned to the schoolhouse clearing he saw the name MAPPO carved on the bark of a tree and, resting underneath it, his friend's machete.

14

A Mysterious Package Arrives on Highfern Row

Everyone moaned about the summer weather and the dismal days of rain. At night, a mist screened Dessie Horgan's jeep and horse-box when he drove along the river road. Mysterious containers were arriving regularly. Main Man was forced to miss his race meetings and visits to the Stony Arms. His skin looked fresher; the vivid redness had faded from his nose and cheeks.

Although Ben tried to ignore what was happening, he always ended up helping the two men unload the containers, then load them back into a different horse-box a few nights later when Eddie Lowe called to pick them up. There was no doubt in Ben's mind that the containers held stolen property. Spirits, cigarettes, electrical goods and leather jackets were being stored in the locked cottage. The horse-box was a clever device to ease suspicion in the unlikely event of someone noticing the arrivals and departures. But only Cathy Dill was likely to see what was happening, and she lived in solitude, in a half-crazy world of cats.

A day's work on Highfern Row, often not ending until the jeep had been loaded or unloaded, left Ben exhausted.

He knew he was being drawn into something over which he had no control and worried continually about Fire Fighter. His determination to clear the hidden field grew stronger.

Yet whenever he found time to visit it, he would stare in dismay at the wilderness. Digging up gorse roots and pulling weeds was slow, damp work. The rain loosened the soil but it also helped the weeds to grow faster, thicker and higher than he would have thought possible. In the entrance facing the road, he began cutting an archway that was high and wide enough to allow his pony to pass through. But he left the shield of branches to hide the opening. Time was scarce and the work slow and laborious. He hacked and dug and cut through the green foliage, honouring Mappo's belief that this secret place would become Jip's haven. It was easier to work within the ruined walls of the cottage. Broken slabs of stone had prevented gorse from rooting and spreading over the floor. This could be Jip's shelter at night. A path had been cleared to the stream where the water ran freely over mossy stones. At times Ben was filled with exhilaration and worked with boundless energy. Sometimes he sat in an exhausted trance, looking around at what he had achieved and wondering at the madness in him that believed the field could be tamed.

The shock of White Heat's disappearance came in the middle of all this activity. Ben heard the news report on the television and watched in disbelief when a replay of the racehorse's most famous victories was shown. The kidnapping had happened at night, despite the heavy security system that surrounded the racehorse's stables. No one heard or saw anything. But at 5 a.m., when his trainer opened the stable-door for an early morning work-out, there was no sign of White Heat.

When Ben visited Craigy's forge later in the evening, the blacksmith was examining a black horse. Ellen Pender was standing beside Dark Sprite. He had imagined seeing her so often, imagined how he would react, what he would say. All he could do was gasp with surprise and stare at her, trying to ignore the jabbing excitement that swept through him.

"Hey Ben. Good to see you," called Craigy. "I believe you and Ellen know each other."

Ellen nodded. Her hands fiddled with Dark Sprite's reins. "I...I just wanted to say...I wanted to apologise for what happened with Douglas. I had hoped to see you but I've been away in boarding school. I'm sorry." Her voice trailed into a whisper of embarrassment.

"What's there to be sorry about?" said Ben. He shrugged and turned to leave. "I'd forgotten all about it till you mentioned it. I'll call back later, Craigy, when you're not busy."

"Come on in, Ben, and stop standing there like a stork. Ellen told me what happened." Craigy placed his arms on the shoulders of both of them, trying to ease the tension. "Sit down there now, the pair of you. You can give a few minutes to an old man who's always looking out for a bit of company."

Ben felt uneasy when Ellen perched beside him on the workbench. But he forgot his discomfort when Craigy produced a newspaper and they scanned the headlines for a report on White Heat. A reward had been offered for information on the horse and the police expected a ransom to be demanded for his safe return. As yet, nothing had been heard from the kidnappers.

"I don't believe there'll be any demand for a ransom," guessed Craigy. "White Heat will be shipped overseas where there'll be a buyer waiting for him. New ownership papers will be forged and no one will be any the wiser. If the police don't catch the thieves, White Heat, as we know him, will disappear forever."

There was something so sad about the idea of never again seeing the magnificent grey in action that they sat silently for a few minutes. Ben became aware of Ellen's arm touching his sleeve and stood up, abruptly. "I have to go. Will I see you around?"

"I might give Dark Sprite a run on the Stretch some morning," she replied. She spoke casually, yet there was a defiant edge to her words, and Ben immediately suspected that her father had forbidden her to ride on Clemartin's Stretch. Then Craigy pointed out something on her horse's foreleg and she went down on her hunkers to examine it. Ben hesitated at the forge entrance. He was still staring at her bent head when she glanced up. Something passed between them.

He did not understand what it was, but it held some sort of shivery electricity and when her eyes flickered away and she touched her lips with her knuckles, the hesitating gesture told him that she was feeling just as confused.

The damp weather continued, muggy grey days with no air to break the humidity. The deliveries of containers had stopped. "I can't oblige any longer," Main Man told Dessie Horgan. For once he was in a good humour, grinning slyly at the jeep driver. "I've other plans. I might be going on a bit of a trip soon."

"Don't tell me you've finally won on the horses, McMullen?" snorted Dessie, not looking at all pleased with this piece of information.

"Never you mind, Horgan. But, as of now, this storage service is going into liquidation."

"You'd be wise to hang loose for a bit longer, McMullen. You never know when we'll need you."

"I'm warning you, Horgan. No more!" Main Man returned to the Stony Arms.

Mr Roche, a representative from Pender's Luxury Developments, was the reason for the dealer's good humour, as Ben discovered the following morning. Mr Roche was immaculately dressed in a pinstriped suit which he brushed fastidiously when he emerged from Main Man's cottage. His sparse hair was lightly oiled and spread carefully across his bald crown.

"It's good to do business with a real gentleman like yourself, Mr Roche." The dealer was beaming as he escorted his visitor to the gate. "This is a prime piece of land and I'm glad we were finally able to fix a price that we could both agree on."

The other man smiled, his thin moustache almost invisible against his upper lip. He offered a limp handshake and winced when his hand was crushed in the dealer's. "Remember now, McMullen. This land deal will be concluded only when Mr Pender can buy the complete stretch of land on Highfern Row."

"You'll have no trouble with that old biddy in the end cottage," said Main Man. "Apart from anything else, those damn moggies are a health hazard. They'd drive a man to drink with their carry-on."

"Yes indeed, it's always handy to have an excuse to

drink," smirked Mr Roche in a prim voice that suggested that nothing stronger than lemonade ever passed his lips. He headed for Cathy Dill's cottage.

Main Man flexed his shoulders with the satisfaction of one of Cathy's cats stretching itself on the blind bridge. "That's Davy Pender's right-hand man. He'd put a well-oiled snake to shame when it comes to business deals. But he's no match for Main Man McMullen. I'll be shaking the dust of this place from my heels soon, pup. So you'd better start thinking of somewhere else to keep that hack."

But Mr Roche did not stay long in Cathy Dill's cottage. Ben heard her front door slam and a cat shriek when the Pender representative kicked it smartly out of his way. A long lock of hair had detached itself from his crown and hung over his forehead. He drove quickly away from Highfern Row and Main Man watched him go, a worried frown on his forehead. "I hope that one up the way is not going to give him any trouble," he muttered.

Ben called into the old woman. She was trembling, holding a cat tightly in her lap.

"He'll be the death of me, Ben," she cried. "I don't want to leave my home. What would my cats do without me to look after them?"

"You don't have to sell your cottage unless you want to, Miss Dill." Ben made her a cup of tea and tried to calm her.

"I've lived here all my life, Ben, before all those people came and took over the fields." She looked like a frightened witch, her grey hair tumbling over her shoulders. Her skin was puckered like fine tissue paper.

"I've a bad feeling in my bones. That man won't give me any rest. Talk talk talk! He told me Main Man has agreed a price for his land with Mr Pender."

"I don't think anything's definite yet." Ben tried to comfort her. "And even if he sells all his cottages, no one can make you sell your home. You live in a free country and you have rights."

She glanced nervously around the room as if she expected Mr Roche with his sleek, pale face to jump out from behind the furniture. The tea cooled in the cup beside her. It was still untouched when Ben left.

But when Mr Roche called again it was to bring bad news. Main Man made no effort to hide his fury. Beads of sweat stood out on his forehead as he listened to the polite voice of Mr Roche outlining his reasons for delaying his purchase of Highfern Row. It had to do with Cathy Dill and some land act that had to be sorted out by the Pender Development team of legal experts. It would delay the purchase of Highfern Row by six months.

Main Man was unable to understand or appreciate such problems. "You can't be serious, Roche. So what if Cathy Dill won't sell?" He was shouting at the top of his voice. "I'm willing to sell and I need the money right now." His voice changed, became wheedling. "It's prime land, Mr Roche. Can't you at least pay me some kind of a deposit?" There was no mistaking his panic. Anything to keep Murty Slomes from his door. But it seemed that Mr Roche was immune to his pleas and he drove off without a backward glance at the dealer, who was shaking his fist at the departing car.

"I'm dead. I'm a dead man," Main Man kept moaning. When he looked at Ben his eyes were glazed as if he could not recognise his surroundings. It was not a bewildered alcoholic haze but real terror that shaped itself into the image of Murty Slomes. Main Man knew it would not take long for the postponement of the land deal to reach the ears of the moneylender and his men. For the rest of the day his eye glanced continually towards the blind bridge.

It had started to rain the following morning when Murty came around the side entrance. He ducked his head in the doorway of the cottage that Ben was mucking out. "Tell that crook, McMullen, to shake a leg. I haven't got all day."

Ben could hear the two men arguing. From the angry sounds, the threatening shouts of Murty, he suspected that the moneylender was demanding the full amount, and was not prepared to leave until it was paid.

"I'm telling you, you'll get it! You know that Davy Pender's interested in buying this land. I'm at a delicate stage of negotiation and you're not helping me, Slomes, with this pressure. He's making me an offer soon. Once that goes through, I'll have more money than I'll know what to do with."

"I'll help you do something with your money, Mr Main Man McMullen. But I'm not waiting another six months for it. You have seven days to pay the outstanding debt. Believe me, McMullen, you can start looking at burial plots if you haven't got it by then."

Main Man's cry sounded like the yelp of a dog whose tail was caught in a doorway. Ben kept well out of his way after Murty left, sensing the violence in the dealer, the need to lash out at anything that stood in his path. Main Man went out early in the afternoon. Ben knew that he was going to Fortune's and that, having lost all his money, he would call into the Stony Arms, wheedling drink from the barman and customers, becoming loud and troublesome until he was finally evicted. Main Man was sinking fast under the pressures of drinking and gambling, of trying to control the impatience of Murty Slomes. For two years he had believed it was just a matter of time before Pender Development made him an offer for his land and he could no longer stand the uncertainty.

Ben stayed on in the cottage, afraid that Main Man might disappear on one of his binges.

"You still here, pup?" At midnight Main Man stood swaying in the doorway. "Was anyone looking for me?" He began to whine, his voice slurring over the words. "Bloodsuckers. That's what they are. And Pender's deliberately driving me round the twist! Why won't he make a decision on my land?"

The hum of an engine on the river road bit into the silence of the night.

Main Man drew back the curtains. "It's Dessie Horgan. I told him…What the hell does he want?" He closed his mouth abruptly and opened the front door. Ben moved to the window and glanced out.

The lights of a jeep lit the row of cottages. In the glare he could see the fat shape of Main Man and Dessie, and, behind them, a large horse-box. When he pushed open the window, he heard Dessie snarling.

"You'll do what you agreed, McMullen, and that's the end of it. I don't care about your plans. We have a deal and you'll stick with it. So shift yourself and get this animal unloaded."

"Animal! What do you mean…animal?" demanded Main Man.

As if answering his question, there was an impatient rap of hooves on the wooden floor of the horse-box. Main Man looked startled, then furious.

"It's a horse," said Dessie. "Yeah yeah...I know it's a change from the usual consignments. But what better place for the beast than this place. You'll have to keep him for a week. I know it's longer than usual but things need to cool off a bit. He'll be collected on the dot."

"A week! You must be off your head!" hissed Main Man. The two men glanced towards the window and lowered their voices.

Eventually, shaping his hand into a fist, Main Man slashed the air with it, then staggered towards the horse-box. He led the horse in through the open entrance at the side and around to the back garden. The dealer was breathing heavily as if he were having a seizure.

White Heat's disappearance was a suspicious thought at the back of Ben's mind when he went outside to inspect the horse.

The same worry had obviously occurred to Main Man. "For a minute there I thought he was trying to unload White Heat on to me," he muttered. His voice still sounded slurred but it was relieved. The stallion, with piebald markings on a rich chestnut-brown coat, bore no resemblance to the famous grey. A white blaze ran down his face and across his nose. Another marking was like a stark map on his back. An extra splash of colour rounded his belly into a plump curve and the white hairs rimming his ankles looked like a crazy zig-zagging pair of socks.

The sound of the jeep's engine died away. "Get that fellow fed and ready for the night, pup. And make sure you put him in the locked cottage. I don't want anyone prying around here. Savvy? And don't even mention him to your shadow! Right!"

"Right, Mr McMullen."

"A week! A flaming week! That's all I need." The back door slammed and silenced Main Man's pathetic voice. Ben led the piebald into the cottage. The animal was docile and sleepy, standing still and making no sound other than a deep sigh when Ben locked the door. Ben knew immediately that the animal had been doped and at the thought, he felt his stomach heave as if he was going to throw up.

On his way home over the blind bridge, he did not see the single headlight of a motorbike blaze for a moment along the river road before stabbing the emptiness of Clemartin's Stretch.

But he heard the roar of the exhaust and paused, his nerves tensed, waiting for the aggressive sound to fade. He shivered. Goosepimples prickled the flesh on his arms. Darkness pressed around him like a sponge, soaking up the secrets of the night.

15

A Challenge on the Stretch

Early next morning Ben cycled to Highfern Row. Main Man was sleeping, snoring loudly, sweating out the fumes of the previous night's whiskey. Ben wrinkled his nose and closed the bedroom door. He approached the locked cottage. The horse, no longer docile, pawed impatiently at the stone floor. The snorting noises carried a grim warning that he was in a state of fear and excitement. He calmed down when Ben opened the door and spoke to him. As the cottage slowly filled with light and his eyes adjusted to the brightness, he allowed Ben to lead him outside.

What would it be like to ride such a powerful animal? The thought was an itch in Ben's mind, refusing to go away. Main Man would not rise until noon. Ben threw caution to the wind and saddled the frisky stallion, who was staring with challenging eyes at the motley occupants of Highfern Row. His presence seemed to make the other horses more dejected, as if his restless energy was a reminder of their age.

Jip whinnied in disapproval until his master ran his fingers through his mane. "It's only a short ride, Jip. I still think you're the greatest. And today I'm going to do some more work on your new home. We're getting out of this place—fast."

Jip licked his hand in forgiveness.

Once out on the Stretch, the stallion settled into a comfortable canter. It was as exhilarating as Ben had expected. Ellen was on the Stretch. She was waiting for him. He knew it and cantered towards her, the wind in his ears, the grass bending before him. She laughed out loud when he passed, then turned her horse around and he heard the sound of hooves, full of excitement and energy, beating in time to his own heart. She galloped past, her face turned for an instant to flash back a triumphant grin. The two horses raced along the flat of Clemartin's Stretch. He allowed his horse to build his stride into an effortless gallop. He had never ridden a horse like this before and knew that he was holding something so powerful that he needed total concentration to control him. Yet he was not frightened. Never had he felt so gloriously free, so happy. He would remember the moment forever. The distance quickly narrowed between him and Ellen. With a wild shout he was past her. He wanted to keep shouting, to let the sound flow on and on.

"That's a fantastic horse you've got," she said when he slowed down and she eventually caught up with him. Her face was full of admiration. She was not at all bothered that the horse had easily outpaced Dark Sprite. Ben grinned back. All the anger and embarrassment of their previous meetings had been lost in the exhilaration of the gallop. When they reached the end of the Stretch, they dismounted. She walked with a long stride, the reins hanging loosely in her hand.

They sat on boulders beside the river and watched the mist gliding over the water.

"Where on earth did Main Man get him?" she asked.

"Some rich customer's going to buy him. I was trying him out for speed before we delivered him today." Ben was uncomfortable with the lie. There was something different about this horse. He was a racer, in a class of his own. Once more he thought about White Heat, feeling his muscles clench with tension before he dismissed the notion. The piebald moved smoothly, stepping daintily over the dewy grass, and began to graze.

"How long have you been working for Main Man?" Ellen asked.

He did a quick calculation, separating the months that seemed to blur into each other. "A year and a half. Too long. But I work for him only because I'm able to keep Jip on Highfern Row." In his voice there was a defensive tone that annoyed him. He did not need to explain anything to Ellen Pender. Yet he continued explaining, justifying, telling her about his house on River View Avenue and Jip's stable and Mr Bricken and the Charney Champs and Mrs Toner. She laughed so much that she almost overbalanced.

"I think that's brilliant!" She wiped her eyes. "I'm just trying to imagine my mother letting me take my horse through our front door. Some hope!" She mimicked a posh accent. It sounded as if she was chewing toffee deep in her throat.

"Ellen, dear, how often must I tell you that your horse is not allowed to sit at table until she learns to hold her knife and fork properly. And while I am on the subject of good table manners, she really must stop eating my flower arrangements for lunch."

Ben told her about Mrs Hackett's Busy Lizzie plant and the way she used to brace herself in front of it when Jip lumbered past. They were still laughing when they remounted for a last gallop before reaching the river road.

"You bastard pup! You're going to feel my fist on your face for this!" Ben heard Main Man's roar before he saw him. But when he looked up it was too late to move. The horse-dealer ran towards them, his jowls wobbling in a way that would have been funny at any other time. Ben was dragged from the horse and felt the crunching force of Main Man's fist on his cheekbone. He staggered back, his fists rising, preparing to fling himself at the horse-dealer. He was no longer a boy to be carelessly bullied. He was a young man, taller than Main Man, supple and strong. When he saw Ellen staring at them, a look of horror on her face, he thought, "Every time she sees me I'm fighting." It made him hesitate just long enough for Main Man to grab the reins from his hand. Without a backward glance, the dealer hurried up the river road, leading the horse around the side entrance of his cottage.

"Are you all right? Lord above, Ben! Are you all right?" They had not heard Cathy Dill opening the gate of her cottage. Her hand was gnarled and brown but her touch was gentle when she laid it against his cheek. The strength of her voice, so out of keeping with her tumbling grey hair and old-fashioned clothes, always surprised Ben.

"Come into the cottage and let me put something on that cheek. It'll be a right swollen mess if you don't."

They followed her into the end cottage. She clapped her hands, shooing cats from above and beneath chairs, offering the young people a seat, then rushed out to the kitchen to get some ice. Ellen sat down gingerly on a dusty armchair with broken springs and gave a little shriek when a cat jumped up on her lap. She relaxed, beginning to stroke the cloudy-grey animal.

"That's Misty," Ben said, tentatively touching his cheek.

"Have they all got names?" Ellen sounded surprised.

"Every one of them. They're her family—"

His words were interrupted by the old woman's return. "There you are now, Ben. Put this on your cheek. It'll take down the swelling." She laid an ice-pack against his face. In the mirror above the fireplace, he inspected the bruise. His eye was already swelling, a puffy red cushion that spread upwards from his cheek. Cathy Dill looked curiously at Ellen. "Are you from around here, child?"

"Not far. I live in Fairview Heights."

The wrinkled face suddenly closed over. She lifted a kitten in her arms and cradled it against her cheek. "You're Davy Pender's daughter, then?"

"Yes. My father is David Pender. Do you know him?"

"Oh I do child. I do." Suddenly Cathy Dill looked very old. "I'm afraid you'll have to leave now. It's feeding time for my cats."

It was obvious that Ellen had been politely dismissed. The old woman walked slowly to the gate with them and whistled through her teeth. Cats came running from the blind bridge and under bushes, to form a straggling procession behind her as she re-entered the cottage.

Ellen glanced back at the open door, frowning. "What got into her, all of a sudden? My father says she's mad, quite bats. Batty Catty." She giggled nervously under Ben's stare. "Isn't that what everyone calls her? I wonder what she'll do with all those cats when she has to leave here?"

"Why should she have to leave? "

"Shhh! Keep your voice down. My father's going to develop this area. And all of Clemartin's Stretch."

"So I heard. But she doesn't have to sell her home if she doesn't want to."

"Don't be silly, Ben. One old woman can't stand in the path of progress. This will be my father's most famous development. He's going to build houses and shops and a huge leisure centre with cinemas and bowling alleys and things like that. It's what Stonyford needs to bring it into the twenty-first century."

Ben tried to imagine it. The river bank road and the row of cottages with their long back gardens would all disappear. Highfern Row would become a busy dual carriageway leading into Clemartin's Stretch. Four-Mile River was also doomed to be channelled into pipes and out of sight, to flow silently underneath the wheels of cars and juggernauts. He thought of Cathy Dill and her cats. They seemed very insignificant in the midst of this vast new land of cement. His anger continued to rise. Ellen was talking, but he no longer heard her words. "Does your father know that he's taking the only home she has ever known?" he asked. His voice was quiet, very cold.

She looked surprised, her mouth poised open on a word. "Can't she live in one of those maisonettes that were built for elderly people in River View? Most of the people who lived in Highfern have moved there."

"But what if she doesn't want to move?"

"Don't be silly, Ben. Who'd want to stay in a dump like that?"

"Cathy Dill would. And your father's breaking up her family."

"Are you calling those cats a family? How ridiculous can you get, Ben Hackett!" She swung herself up on Dark Sprite and sat, looking down at him, a splash of colour on each cheek. "When that woman moves my father will make sure that she's well looked after." Her tone was snooty and defiant. Ben did not bother replying and, when she rode down the river road, Ellen's back was as straight as a ramrod.

"Has that rich brat left?" Main Man demanded when he returned. He glared at Ben's swollen cheek. "That'll teach you to meddle in things that don't concern you. You don't mess around with deliveries. I've warned you before. You're paid to run this kip. Nothing else. Savvy!" He moved restlessly around the kitchen, looking at his watch every few minutes as if he was unable to keep track of time or reality. "Haven't I got enough worries without being landed with this. No one cares about my problems." Main Man was in a mood of self-pity, a state that normally followed a heavy bout of whiskey-drinking.

Ben spent the next hour grooming the piebald. "Where did you come from?" he wondered. "And where on this miserable earth are you going?"

16

Main Man's Departure

Horse-buyers converged on the river road. Sunshine sparkled on the moist tyre tracks along the banks of Four-Mile River. The experienced buyers looked at Main Man and read his anxiety. Word had spread that the dealer was selling his animals in a hurry. Main Man tried to bargain but his blustering personality was missing and when a price was finally agreed, it was always lower than the horse's worth.

Throughout the sale, the piebald had remained locked in the cottage, sprawled on the floor in a drug-induced stupor. Ben felt his stomach churning with disgust every time he looked at the piebald. When the dealers and travellers and knackers and Taggy Somers finally departed, only Jip and the hidden horse remained.

Next morning Main Man rolled down the window of his van and leaned out. "I'll be away for the day. If anyone comes asking for me, tell them I'll see them tomorrow." He licked his tongue over dry lips. "And tell that bloodsucker Murty Slomes to keep his wig on. He'll get his money when I return. OK, pup?"

"Are you going to a race meeting?" Ben asked.

The dealer's eyes narrowed. "I've to meet a few of the lads at the Curragh. Don't fret, pup. I know what I'm doing."

"If you didn't spend all your money drinking and gambling you'd be able to pay off Murty Slomes. You're a mess, McMullen. A blubber-bellied mess!" Ben clenched his fists, challenging Main Man to get out of the van.

Main Man smiled. It was an ugly twist in his battered face, revealing small, yellow teeth. "I'll see to you when I get back, pup. Never fear. But I've more important things to do for the moment."

"What about that horse?" Ben demanded. "What happens if you don't get back before tomorrow night in time for Eddie Lowe to collect him?"

"Stop worrying. I'll be back by tonight. Just keep him out of sight. If I hear word that you've been galloping him on the Stretch, I'll skin you alive."

Ben opened the padlocked door of the locked cottage where the horse had remained hidden. Although the effects of the drug were wearing off, he staggered when he emerged into daylight. In the week since he arrived at the cottage, he had lost weight. He was restless in the confined space. Just like the leather jackets and the cartons of cigarettes and the crates of spirits that moved through Highfern Row, someone had stolen this horse and he was now in Ben's hands, on the halfway stage of his journey. If Fire Fighter called, Ben could be arrested as a receiver of stolen goods. The thought sent shivers of panic down his back. Every instinct told him that Main Man would not return, that he would bet all his money and lose. Ben wanted to set the horse free to be picked up by someone. Yet if the dealer did return he would have

Horgan and Lowe, as well as Main Man, to deal with. That thought was even more terrifying than anything Fire Fighter could do to him.

Tomorrow night Eddie Lowe would arrive and Ben would depart with Jip from Highfern Row. The field was not ready. But the path to the river was clear. Maybe the Charney Champs would help. The soccer season would start again in August and, if they wanted to end up on top of the league, they had better start taking care of their mascot.

When it was obvious that Main Man was not going to return that night, he rang his mother to tell her that he was staying overnight in Highfern Row.

"Who did you say you were?" she asked in the posh voice she normally kept for Mrs Toner. "Ben Hackett! Who's that? Oh, now I remember. You're the Ben Hackett who used to live at 16 River View Avenue?"

Ben sighed and held the phone some distance from his ear.

"Would you mind telling me what you're doing over in that dump?" she demanded, reverting to her normal voice. Her anxiety seemed to vibrate down the telephone wire. "It was a bad day's luck when you bought Jip from that slick-fisted crook."

From the third cottage Ben heard the impatient call of the piebald. "Stop worrying, Ma. I'll see you tomorrow night and this time I'll be home for good. I've found a new place for Jip."

The roar of a motorbike mounting the blind bridge and the indignant screech of cats when their night-time prowling was disturbed, made an uneasy sound-track for his dreams.

Murty Slomes came storming around the side entrance of Main Man's cottage the following morning.

"Where is he?" He was like a bull, poised to charge, neck lowered, glaring at Ben. "Tell Mr Main Man McMullen that I want his fat ass out here this instant."

"He's not here, Slomes. But he'll be back later if you want me to give him a message."

"I suppose there wouldn't be any truth to the rumour that your boss has done a runner? That he was seen yesterday at the Curragh races and in a pub in Newbridge afterwards, crying into a glass of whiskey." He pressed his face close to Ben. "You wouldn't know anything about that, I suppose?"

"No...no I don't." Ben moved away from him and pointed to Main Man's cottage. The piebald, locked securely in the third cottage, was staying quiet, as if he sensed the fury of the bull-like man, who seemed capable of pawing the ground with his foot at any moment. "Main Man's coming back today. Everything's still here...his furniture...and...and—" Ben gulped and decided it was wiser to stay silent.

"Where are all the animals?" demanded Murty. "This garden is normally full of hacks." Jip had wandered out of sight behind a high bush and was contentedly grazing.

"Trade's been slow. But look in his cottage. All his stuff's still there."

Murty opened the kitchen door. Everything in the cottage was in place. Main Man's clothes were strewn across his bedroom floor. The moneylender gave a loud snort, then slammed the door behind him. Jip had emerged from behind the tree to stare at Murty, his ears pricked, tensing his body when the man gave his rump an angry wallop. "That hack's a tube of glue if I ever saw one. As for that junk inside! It wouldn't fetch tuppence in a jumble sale. If that bastard's done a runner, we'll hunt him down and feed his carcase to the dogs. No one, but no one, messes Murty Slomes around…especially when it's a matter of £25,000, with interest."

Ben whistled in surprise. He knew Main Man was in deep with Murty Slomes. But not that deep.

"I'll be back in a few hours. So tell your boss to stay put until I call or there'll be an army out looking for him."

The piebald was like a weight crushing Ben's chest. After Murty left, he gave a whinnying roar, the most powerful, primitive sound Ben had ever heard, high-pitched, filled with terror and rage. Since Main Man's departure, Ben had fed the horse without adding the narcotics that the dealer kept locked in a tin box, hidden in a ledge of the kitchen chimney. For the first time since his gallop on Clemartin's Stretch, the horse was fully alert and full of fear. Ben was afraid to release him in case he attacked Jip. Yet he could not stand the sound of the piebald's terror.

When the horse started kicking the locked cottage door, Ben knew that the rotting wood was only a frail barrier that would easily shatter. He took a deep breath and released it harshly through his nostrils, frightened that he would be unable to control the horse. Since starting to work for Main Man he had felt his link with the horses beginning to weaken, being gradually stifled by the atmosphere on Highfern Row. Now, as the key turned in the padlock, he began to make his strange sounds, no longer frightened, every nerve in his body trying to understand and calm the horse. His voice did not rise but despite the noise and the terror that came from behind the closed door, it made itself heard. Ben entered the cottage.

The windows had been boarded up but he could see the broad outline of the horse, tensed, ready to attack if Ben's voice faltered. When he felt the steady hands of the young man on his neck, the piebald trembled. He was docile but nervous when Ben led him into the garden into the shade of overhanging trees. Jip, sensing the dominance of the piebald, moved swiftly out of the way.

"Hello Ben!" said a low, very subdued voice behind him. He sprang back from the horse, spun around to face Ellen Pender.

She was wearing trainers and shorts and an over-sized sweatshirt that carried a picture of a whale with a harpoon buried in its side. The lettering underneath it read, "*Stop Mainlining the Whale.*"

"It's OK, I'm not a ghost." She grinned. "Even if you did think I was one once." Her smile faded when she recognised the piebald. "What's that horse doing here? I thought there was a buyer arriving for him last week."

"The deal fell through." Ben spoke abruptly. "He's being collected tonight." His hands shook and he shoved them into his jeans pocket so that she would not notice. But her attention had already shifted to his eye. The skin around it had faded to a mucky-yellow.

"Your eye still looks awful."

"Did you tell anyone about what happened to me last week?" he asked, touching his face, trying to sound casual.

Her voice sank to a whisper, sharing his nervousness. "I never said a word. I wasn't supposed to be on the

Stretch so I was petrified that Main Man would tell my father. I wanted to call in during the week and see how you were. But until this morning Main Man's van was always outside. And there were all those caravans and horse-boxes! How can you stay working for him, after what he did to you?"

"I'll be gone after tonight."

"That's good, Ben. This place is a real dump. The sooner it's knocked down the better."

"So you said the other day."

"Yeah. Well...I...I wanted to say I'm...ah, I'm sorry for being such a bitch then." Her words rushed together. "I've been thinking about what you said and I had no right to dismiss the old woman like that, or to say she was crazy. I suppose I couldn't imagine anyone wanting to stay around here!" She shrugged. "So...I'm sorry."

As always, her casual way of dismissing everything old as a dump that would become fodder for her father's army of bulldozers, made him angry. But he never managed to stay mad at her for long. He thought about her so often, seeing her face with such clarity that he sometimes felt he could reach out and touch it. Daft loving. He shook off the image his mother's words created.

"It's my birthday today, Ben. I'm sixteen."

"Happy birthday. I remember your fourteenth one very well."

"How come?" She looked puzzled. He told her about his visit to Fairview Heights. "That was some present your father gave you. Did he make it back on time for your party?"

"What do you think?" She shook her head. "It was a

week before I saw him again. So what! My parents are always telling me that I'm the luckiest girl in the world. When I think about it, it's all due to the fact that my father is such a busy man. I'm having a party tonight. Do you want to come along?" It was a casual invitation but she blushed as she gave it.

"You must be joking!" He stepped back a pace, surprised at the suggestion. "I suppose this is a personal gilt-edged invitation from your father."

"It's my birthday." She sounded defiant. "I can ask any friend I like. My father told me so."

"But you and I know what your father told me the last time we met. I was to keep to my own side of the river, away from his daughter."

"Oh, come on! That happened a year ago and you told me you'd forgotten about it. Anyway, there'll be so many people at the party, he won't even notice you."

"I'm not hiding in a crowd to please you!"

Ellen touched his arm. "That's not what I meant, Ben. I don't want you to hide in a crowd. My father was wrong to take sides. Sometimes when he loses his temper he says things he doesn't mean. Let's forget about that day. Please. I'd like us to be friends."

He shrugged, smiling suddenly, his face relaxing. "All right. We're friends. What do we do now?"

The pressure of her fingers seemed to melt into his arm. "Come to my party. Meet some of my friends. They're not all like Douglas."

"Ellen, I can't. I've to work here tonight. Maybe some other time."

"If you say so." She did not seem surprised at his refusal. "I suppose I'd better go. I've loads to do yet." She glanced curiously at the piebald. "Is he the reason you have to stay here?"

Ben nodded.

"Who is Main Man going to sell him to?"

"I don't know. All I care about is that he'll be gone by tonight and I can leave here."

"Where will you bring Jip?"

"I've found a place. A secret place."

"Really? Where is it? Go on, Ben, tell me."

She had extended an invitation to her party which she must have known he would refuse. But it had opened an avenue between them, created the exciting possibility of them doing things together. Suddenly he found it difficult to catch his breath. "Would you really like to see it?"

His arm felt warm when she removed her hand. "Tell me where it is and I'll meet you there tomorrow."

From the river road, they heard Dark Sprite whinnying. The sound seemed to come from a great distance. Ben arranged to meet her at the blind bridge, stumbling over the words.

Once more her horse whinnied. "I really had better go." Her laugh was a breathy gasp. At the side entrance he called her name. She paused and looked back.

"Happy birthday, Ellen."

She grinned, flapped her hand in a lazy wave. "See you tomorrow on the blind bridge, Ben."

17

Saying Farewell on the Blind Bridge

Throughout the day, Diver, one of Murty's strong-arm men, kept watch from a car that was parked on the river road, in full view of the cottages. Main Man did not return.

It was after ten that night when Ben discovered that his pony was missing. Jip had spotted a weak link in the hedge barrier and trampled it down. Since moving back to Highfern Row, Jip had not tried to break through the fencing. Perhaps it was the presence of the stallion that had made him restless and revert to his old habits but, when Ben went outside, he could see only one horse, the mysterious piebald. Only half an hour had passed since Ben had seen Jip. The old pony was a slow mover and would not have wandered very far.

Ben led the piebald back into the cottage, loaded up a hay manger and locked the door before setting off in pursuit of Jip. The black car was also missing. Diver had obviously given up hope of Main Man's return and driven away. When the lights lit the river road, and the river mist formed a hazy orange glow around them, Ben thought that one of Murty's men was returning for a night-shift watch. But it was Eddie Lowe who stepped down from a white jeep with a horse-box attached. He groaned when he heard that Main Man was not in his cottage.

"That good-for-nothing dipso!" he hissed. "When do you expect him back?"

"He should be back soon." Ben was beginning to sound like a parrot. As if anticipating his release, the piebald snorted loudly. Eddie jerked his head, nervously. "Why doesn't he hire a brass band and let the world know where he is?" His shoulders were tense and he flexed them in a circular movement, blowing his breath loudly through puckered lips. "I've had a pig of a drive and I'm starving. I suppose Main Man wouldn't have anything in the fridge?"

"He hasn't even got a fridge," Ben said. "And there's nothing in the cottage, except some stale bread and butter. There might be some cheese..."

"No, thank you very much," said Eddie, shuddering fastidiously. "A good plate of fish and chips or a curry— I'd sink my teeth into that all right. What's the village like for takeaways?"

"The Chinese takeaway does a good curry but it's always packed at this hour of the night," said Ben.

"What about that takeaway van that used to park on River View. Is it still there?"

"It is," replied Ben. "And the fish and chips are better than anything you'll get in the village."

"That sounds like a good idea to me," said Eddie. "Listen, kid. I'll go across the bridge and pick up something there. Have that animal ready when I return. There's an anxious buyer who's been kept waiting for his package longer than the terms of agreement." Eddie Lowe laughed abruptly. Mist swirled around him when he paused underneath a lamppost to light a cigarette. He sat in the driver's seat, flicking cigarette ash from the window. "See you in half an hour, kid," he yelled.

The jeep moved down the river road. Ben began to shake, as if something clammy had walked over his skin. Sweat trickled down his back and under his arms. It felt cold against his forehead. He could not understand his terror as he watched the tail-lights of the horse-box disappear over the blind bridge.

On Clemartin's Stretch, he called Jip's name, pitching his voice in a shrill greeting that the pony would instantly recognise. But there was no answering whinny. It was impossible to see in the darkness but he knew that Jip's hearing was keen and that he would immediately answer Ben's voice. The throb of a motorbike engine was a distant sound but, otherwise, there was silence on the Stretch. When he returned to the river road, there was still no sign of the pony.

Thirty minutes had passed. Eddie would be back soon. As if in answer to his thoughts, he heard the strain of the jeep, responding to the green traffic light, climbing in low gear towards the blind arch.

Ben heard another sound, the gunning roar of an engine, and a gust of air rushed past him. The motorbike, emerging from Clemartin's Stretch, raced along the narrow road and turned sharply towards the blind bridge. Ben saw the shape of the biker crouched over the handlebars. A tinted glass visor covered his face and there was a pillion passenger on the back. Jeep headlights began to flare. In that same instant, as Ben stood petrified on the river road, he saw the silhouette of Jip, framed on the summit of the bridge. Then he was aware only of fragmented images; of screams, a thin sound of terror from the pillion passenger, hands over ears, a banner of black hair, and Jip, a blurred hulk, hypnotised by the approaching headlights. The biker climbed the blind bridge, ignoring the red traffic light, seeing Jip at the last second.

Eddie Lowe's jeep reached the summit in that same instant. When the biker swerved in a crazy zig-zag, the exhaust belched noise and black smoke. With a last desperate crazy swerve the biker avoided the pony and the jeep, then vanished over the hump of the bridge like a black arrow heading towards the wastelands. Ben felt no sense of surprise when the night exploded around him.

The jeep, made difficult to control by the horse-box it was pulling, spun to a jangled screech of metal, steam hissing, stones flying as it skidded against both sides of the blind bridge. When Ben reached the jeep, Eddie Lowe's body was slumped, his warm hands still clenched on the steering wheel.

Jip screamed once, tossed his head and lay still as Ben ran towards him.

"Help me...help me...help me!" he kept whispering, tearing himself away from his pony's side and running towards the telephone in Main Man's cottage.

The emergency phone number was answered immediately. Ben gasped out the message and ran back to the blind bridge. Sirens sounded. Blue lights whirled. Headlights dazzled, breaking the black night like some scattered constellation that had fallen to earth. An ambulance stopped at the foot of the bridge and men began working on the wreckage of the jeep. It took a long time to cut Eddie Lowe free. Then the ambulance siren screamed a warning and headed towards Stonyford Village. Meanwhile Ben returned to Jip. The pony's eyes were open but clouding over with a haze of bewilderment.

"Oh Jip!" Ben lay on the ground beside him, pressed his face against the soft belly. Then he could hear no other sound except the drumming call of a heartbeat, the heartbeat of his horse growing louder, louder until it filled his mind and his own heart was beating to the same rhythm. His breath changed, deepened, belonging to the mysterious force flowing between him and his dying animal, the bond that had united them since the first time they met on the wastelands. Then there was only his own breath and his own heartbeat.

Jip's blood was running cold as he lay on the hump of the blind bridge and Ben let his tears trickle into the mangy, speckled coat. The words that came to his lips had no meaning. They were whispers that told of love and loss and when he knew that words were no longer necessary, he wept in the shadow of the crumbling walls, feeling empty, as if everything he knew was slipping away from him.

"You've got to let him go, Ben." Craigy's hands were an anchor, helping him to his feet. "Come away with me now and let these people do their job."

Photographers from the papers had gathered, clicking their cameras at the mangled jeep and broken horse-box. A tow-truck removed the wreckage and cleared a passage over the bridge. When a large truck rounded the hump and Ben saw black lettering on the side, spelling out the name Canine Chops, he ran towards it, shouting, his hands waving it away, as if he could physically force it back over the bridge.

"Get that truck out of here immediately," roared Craigy. Taggy Somers tried to explain that he had been only following orders and normally the factory took care of all dead carcases.

"This is a precious animal we're talking about. Not a carcase," Craigy continued to roar. The shock of his anger calmed and silenced Ben. "I'm going to organise the pony's removal. I'm taking care of everything. Understand?"

Taggy nodded and hurried back into his truck.

"What'll happen to Jip?" asked Ben.

"I've had a word with the lads who have the lifting equipment," replied Craigy. "They're going to use their truck to take him away. We'll bury him tonight."

"Don't bury him on Clemartin's Stretch?" Ben whispered. "They'll be digging it up soon and I don't want him to be disturbed, ever again."

"I've a little bit of land at the back of the forge. It's peaceful, shaded by trees and the birds nest there in the spring. That's where we'll lay him to rest," Craigy promised.

The mist had cleared. Purple clouds darkened the moon. Four-Mile River ran calmly under the blind bridge. Ben watched the lights of the truck approach as two men and Craigy prepared to do their grim work. He was still dazed by the speed with which everything had occurred. But in the strange way that people accept the unthinkable once it happens, Jip had slipped into a place in his mind called memory where he would never be forgotten.

18

A Secret in the Hidden Field

When the phone rang Ben jumped with shock. Since the accident he had been sitting by the kitchen window of Main Man's cottage watching dawn settle over the gardens of Highfern Row, remembering the brown eyes of the old pony, the feel of his shaggy mane tangling in his fingers.

"Listen kid, I've been hearing a news report on the radio throughout the night about an accident in your neck of the woods with a horse and a jeep." Dessie Horgan, the delivery driver, sounded panic-stricken. "Eddie's not turned up yet and all hell's breaking loose. So I just thought I'd enquire. Quick lad, get Main Man fast until I talk to him."

"He's gone."

"Gone! What do you mean—gone?"

"He disappeared two days ago. And that accident...it...it was Eddie! He's been brought to hospital in a coma."

Dessie Horgan gasped, cursed, raged and finally wept. Ben could not decide if the tears were caused by fear, temper or remorse over Eddie's accident. He waited in silence until Dessie's voice was steady again. "If Main Man wasn't there last night when all this happened, then who the hell was dealing with Eddie?"

"Me."

There was a pause as if Dessie was afraid to ask the next question. "What-about-the-horse-what-happened-to-his-body?" He spoke with precision and Ben could almost feel the tension behind the question.

"He's been buried...my pony..." Ben was unable to continue.

"Buried!"

The sharp exclamation managed to penetrate the sadness surrounding Ben. His mind moved, slapped into action by the panic in Dessie's voice. Dessie Horgan thought that the piebald had died on the blind bridge.

"Yes, Mr Horgan. The horse has been buried. I arranged everything. He's buried at the back of a blacksmith's forge."

"Have the police been involved?"

"No. A friend organised it."

"Whew! That's a relief. But what a waste...what a bloody waste." Suddenly Dessie sounded as if he was crying again. He cleared his throat. "Main Man always said you could be trusted and that dipso wouldn't normally trust his own shadow. You did well, Ben. You'll be paid for your troubles when all this fuss dies down. But for the moment, I want you to do us all a favour. The piebald never existed. OK? If anyone asks, it was one of Main Man's hacks and you'd just bought it. No one's going to suspect otherwise."

Ben put back the receiver, his head swimming.

"What to do? What to do? What to do?" By some unwanted and unasked-for miracle, Ben had another horse. This time no one was going to take him away. He must be hidden, fast. If Main Man returned, the truth would come out and another man would replace Eddie Lowe, another horse-box would drive away from Highfern Row.

Once Ben's decision had been made, he moved fast. His limbs seemed wired to some distant command, not really part of his body any longer. His mind felt equally detached. Outside, all was quiet. The cats had returned to the blind bridge and dozed on the crumbling walls. Morning would bring the police back again. By then they would have discovered the identity of Eddie Lowe and would start searching the cottages. They had questioned Ben soon after the accident but, even though he was dazed with grief, some protective instinct made him shake his head and tell them that Eddie had been looking for Main Man and had driven off without leaving a name.

There was no time to lose. Tyre marks darkened the surface of the blind bridge. There were bricks scattered about where the walls had been broken through. He tightened his stomach muscles and clenched his teeth, urging the horse over the arch. The horse quivered, hesitated, pulling his head against Ben, sensing the presence of death. But he calmed down and responded to the commanding voice.

A sprawling mountain of old fridges, stale food and plastic wrappings had been left to settle on the rubbish tip. Sea gulls screeched and fought each other, trying to claim the choicest pickings.

Since Ben had last visited the field, the thick ferns and weeds had increased. He hacked out a path for the horse with the machete, ignoring scratches and stings and the rustling sounds beneath his feet. The cracking snap of dead wood terrified him. Surely someone would come along to see what was causing so much noise. But no voices shouted. They penetrated deeper and deeper into the tangled growth.

He hammered a stake into the ground and unwound the long length of rope from around his shoulders. The horse would have space to wander as far as the stream.

"I'll be back as soon as I can," Ben whispered. "Now that you're mine, I suppose I'd better give you a name." Apart from the wild gallop across Clemartin's Stretch a week before, he had not built up any relationship with the piebald. All his love had belonged to Jip. He stroked the horse's muzzle, trying to share some of that love. But it was too soon. The words that normally flowed so easily from him were missing. He wanted a horse. But it was not the same yearning that had swept over him the first time he had mounted Jip's back. This was a hard desire for something that others bought so easily, without having to worry about cost or shelter.

If Jip had been allowed to stay in the Hacketts' back garden, he would be alive, sleeping securely in his stable. Ben could not bear to think about this and left the horse, unable to think of a suitable name.

He felt his way blindly. Briars tripped him and ferns brushed against his cheeks. When he reached the wastelands he was exhausted. Red embers of wood sank into the dying fire that had blazed through the night. Danny Moone lay snoring beside it, his thin body hunched into the warmth of his jacket. At seventeen he already had the beaten face of an old man. No one was ever going to make Ben Hackett look like that. He straightened his shoulders, looking down at the friend who had shared his earliest years. It seemed like yesterday. It seemed like a lifetime ago. "Come on, Danny. I'm bringing you home." He tried to waken Danny, whose eyes opened in a glazed stare as he tried to focus on the face above him.

"Ah piss off, Ben!" he muttered without any emotion and slid back into his cider-filled dreams.

The police called to River View a few hours later. Fire Fighter questioned him about the accident and asked why Eddie Lowe had been at Main Man's cottage. Eddie was a crook, Fire Fighter informed him. Not a big time crook, just someone who picked up mysterious packages in the dead of night and never asked any questions.

"What was he doing at Highfern Row?" Fire Fighter glanced keenly at Ben, who looked sullenly down at his feet. "Was he dumping something?"

"He just called to talk to Main Man. But he didn't hang around once he heard Main Man had gone away for a few days."

"Run away would be more appropriate," snapped Fire Fighter. "Don't hold your breath waiting for that villain to return. If there's anything that you should tell me, Ben, now's your chance. Tomorrow may be too late."

Ben shook his head and said nothing.

"Well then, perhaps you can give us a description of the motorbike that mounted the bridge at the same time as the jeep."

Again Ben shook his head, stood up and moved restlessly around the small kitchen. He wanted to give an answer, to describe every last detail of the machine that had torn such a hole in his life. But all he could remember was its speed, a blurred image of crouching black figures and a voice, screaming.

The Charney Champs were in tears when they called to the Hacketts' house. Susie carried a wreath of red and gold-yellow roses, tied with an enormous black bow. She insisted on visiting Jip's grave. Craigy's garden was just a small wedge of land at the back of the forge, big enough for one tree and a few rows of flowers. The flowers had been uprooted, replaced by a mound of earth.

In front of Craigy's astonished eyes, the Charney Champs crowded around the grave and sang their team song.

"We're going to be relegated next season. I just know it," wept Susie Moone. "Now that Jip's gone, it'll be like Broomhill all over again." (In pre-Jip days they had been defeated 10-0 by Broomhill.)

"No it won't," said Craigy. "Jip was your lucky mascot but he didn't help you to win your matches. He just gave you the confidence to believe you were invincible. Make no mistake, girls. It was your own skills that scored every winning goal. With or without a mascot, you're the greatest."

The Charney Champs looked disbelieving but pleased.

"Isn't Craigy a little dote?" breathed Susie into Ben's ear when they left Forge Alley. "I'm going to start the team training immediately. The summer break is over!"

Ben returned to Highfern Row that evening to collect horse concentrate food from the store. He knew immediately that the police had been searching the cottages and gardens, rifling through the sacks of oats and grains in the store-room. They had forced open the locked door of the third cottage and it hung from one hinge, creaking eerily, swinging to and fro. Cathy Dill's cats swarmed over the gardens, arching their backs against the walls of the empty white washed stables. Already there was a desolate look about the place. When Ben tried to imagine Jip, he could no longer picture him beneath the trees.

At the gate he looked towards Clemartin's Stretch, at the tract of land spreading out from the river road. What memories. Suddenly he remembered that he had arranged to meet Ellen Pender and bring her to the hidden field. Until that moment, he had completely forgotten about her. He wondered if she had turned up, unaware that Jip had been killed.

When he saw her riding Dark Sprite along the river road, he was convinced, for an instant, that she was a figment of his imagination. She averted her eyes when she reached the junction in the river road leading over the blind bridge, as if she could not bear to look at the scorched tyre marks on the surface. Then she saw him and sat very still on Dark Sprite.

Ben was surprised at her appearance. Her face was red and blotchy from tears that must have been cried through the night. She dismounted with a clumsy movement, clinging to the horse as if she was terrified the animal would bolt on her. Ben moved towards her, ready to catch her if she fell. But she regained her balance and walked slowly towards him.

"Oh Ben! I can't believe it...I can't believe this has happened...tell me it didn't happen? Please...please."

Her voice trailed away when he shook his head, unable to answer her. "I'm sorry! I'm so sorry." She put her arms around him and, before he knew what he was doing, his arms reached out in a clumsy, half-blind gesture and pulled her close against him. He wanted to bury himself in the softness of her skin. If he moved his head he could touch her lips and kiss her.

Instead he kissed her hair, private kisses that she could not feel, breathing in the fresh scent of her skin.

But there was something wrong. Her body was tense, withdrawing itself from him. When she pulled away, he saw her tears. There was an ugly sound to her sobbing, like a child who had started, but did not know how to stop this avalanche of weeping.

"What is it?" he asked, pushing her hair back from her face. Her forehead felt hot, fever-heat, and her thick fringe was lank beneath his fingers. "That must have been some party last night." He tried to lighten his voice.

It was the wrong thing to say. Roughly, as if unable to bear his touch, she clambered up on Dark Sprite's back with that same clumsy urgency and rode away.

He watched her until she was out of sight then forced himself to walk over the blind bridge on his way home to River View. The sun lit the stonework, covered with a jagged rust-coloured stain. Something flashed, something small, fiercely reflecting the sun's rays. He knelt down, believing it to be a piece of metal from the jeep, and picked up a gold earring, a tiny, perfectly carved star with a precious stone studded in the centre. It rested in his hand. Without thinking he flung it into Four-Mile River. He watched it ripple the water and sink out of sight.

19

Murty's Midnight Call

Two weeks passed with Ben in a state of limbo. He bitterly regretted his decision to hide the horse. Under his breath he kept repeating, "I must have been mad. I must have been off my head!"

He was reluctant to give the horse a name, but each time he visited the field, the piebald responded to the sound of his call, whinnying an excited greeting whenever he heard the swish of leaves in the passageway. Restless and highly-strung, the horse needed space to work off his energy. It was too risky to bring him to the Stretch so Ben could exercise him only along the path that he had cleared to the stream. The store of food in Highfern Row would soon run out and he needed money to feed the horse. A long trudge to the factories on the industrial estate began. Security men handed him application forms and little comfort. "We'll put you on file and let you know if anything turns up."

Then he heard that Pender Luxury Development were looking for casual labour. The foreman on one of the sites was a friend of Mr Hackett and was hopeful that Ben would get a few months' work. "It'll mostly be shifting rubbish from the sites and running odd jobs for the men. I'll start you next Monday."

On Friday night he called to the Hacketts' house. "I don't understand it, but it's a no-go situation. I've orders from the top not to give you any work. It seems that you had a bit of a run-in with the boss. That wasn't a wise move, Ben, not a wise move at all."

Since he moved the horse, Ben no longer visited the forge. He knew that Craigy missed him, but the old man's eyes were as sharp as razor blades and Ben was afraid of blurting out the truth. One evening, Craigy called to his house to offer him part-time work in the forge. Another new riding school was opening about two miles from Stonyford and business was expanding. "Look at me, past retirement age by more than a few years and I've never been busier," boasted the old man. He looked eagerly at Ben. "I'm thinking of taking on a partner. You have an understanding of animals that I've never known in anyone else. But I've seen it fade since you started working for Main Man. It's as if that dealer put a clamp on your heart and you just won't allow yourself to feel any more. Don't let that gift die, Ben. Why not work part-time with me and go back to school again? You've the brains but, what's more important, you have the ability to do something really worthwhile with your life. You could work with animals, become a vet...or a horse trainer or...the sky's the limit. There's no reason why you can't, now is there?" It was a long speech for Craigy and he paused to draw breath, gazing expectantly at Ben, who stared blankly back at him. "Is anything wrong, lad?" He put his hand on Ben's shoulder.

"Nothing's wrong. I just haven't got time to drop into

the forge the way I used to. And I've stopped being interested in horses."

"I don't believe you. Something's wrong and you're afraid to tell me. I've just got this to say and then I'm leaving you alone. You know where the forge is. I'll be there when you're ready to talk to me."

He had never known a friend like Craigy. His throat felt raw after the old man left. Twilight was falling over the back garden and the twins' pigeons rustled their feathers, swooping in and out of the stable that had become their home. Ben drew in deep lungfuls of air. He had wanted to listen to Craigy but his mind was closed to anything other than the hidden field and the next visit he would make to it.

That night he was still awake when he heard the hall door being forced open with what seemed like the force of a battering-ram. He was out of bed and in a crouching position of defence before he fully realised what was happening. Running downstairs, wearing only pyjama-bottoms, he saw the frightened faces of his sisters, Cindy and Jean, at the door of their bedroom. Dave and Steve stumbled behind him. He heard the bewildered sobs of his baby sister, Maria, his father shouting and, above everything, the roars of Murty Slomes.

"Get the horse, lads. Go straight through the kitchen. Hurry! Hurry!"

Mrs Hackett was in her nightdress, beating Murty with her fists. Murty pushed her away and she fell, hitting her head against the side of the stairs. Ben had never seen such fury on his father's face as when he jumped at Murty. The two men began to fight in the hall.

"There's no horse here!" Cindy kept screaming. "Get

out of our house!" She helped her mother to her feet. When Ben reached the back garden, Diver and another man had kicked open the stable-door.

"Get that horse or Murty'll make us swing," yelled the second man. Flocks of startled pigeons scattered in a flurry of dust and feathers, flapping their wings blindly in the faces of the men.

"Are you satisfied?" Ben yelled. "There's no horse here."

"Hooligans," shrieked Mrs Toner, standing on a chair and looking into the garden. "You Hacketts still think you're living in a city centre slum!"

She fell off her chair, tumbling backwards when some of the pigeons swooped low over her head. Diver brushed furiously at the swirling birds while trying to dislodge Steve, who was clinging, piggy-back style, to his shoulders.

"Get that little scab off my back!" He roared at his companion, who grabbed the boy's legs and dragged him to the ground. Steve wriggled from his grip and stood, fists clenched, a twelve-year-old pugilist, ready to take on the world of Murty Slomes.

Diver advanced, shoulders lowered. Steve fled.

"I said get the horse, not play chasing," roared Murty, who had left Mr Hackett clutching his left eye and counting stars.

"I'm phoning the police and the corporation and the church and the newspapers and the Bird Protection Society and...and...the Government!!" Mrs Toner was back up on her chair again, her nose red with excitement, rollers like beer-cans giving her head the appearance of a corrugated roof.

Ben was lifted, dragged by Murty into the stable and

pressed against the wall.

"Where's the horse?" hissed Murty. "You've hidden a valuable animal and I want him. I want him fast, like right now!"

"I don't know what you're talking about. There were no horses left. Main Man sold them all."

"Is that a fact, now! Then how come McMullen had a different story to tell us?" Murty began to speak fast, saliva spraying Ben's face. In the suffocating atmosphere of the stable, where Jip had once lived so contentedly, Ben listened in growing terror. Main Man had been found. Murty and his men were experts when it came to finding "scurriers," their name for anyone who tried to renege on a debt by going into hiding.

Main Man had felt safe in a caravan on a remote strand in Donegal, surviving on bottles of whiskey and tins of canned soup. At night he emerged to use the phone in a quiet village pub, calling in favours, trying to wheedle, bribe and beg enough money to approach Murty again; to stave off the moneylender until David Pender bought his land. He had been hiding out for two weeks when he rang Dessie Horgan and heard about the accident on the blind bridge. That night, Murty and his men found him. Ben could almost hear the dealer's frightened curses, the noise of the caravan door shuddering open under the impact of Murty's shoulder. When Main Man had been beaten senseless, Murty flung a bucket of water over him.

Main Man spluttered into consciousness, sobbing, "I wasn't on the run from you, Murty. I swear it. I just couldn't go back to Highfern Row..."

"But only because you knew I was waiting with a bag

for your guts, McMullen."

Main Man cringed away from the moneylender. "I couldn't go back...I'd...Slomes, you don't know what happened. I wasn't there..."

"You were never there! Too busy gambling other people's money."

"No, no. It wasn't that. Eddie Lowe..." Main Man was finding it difficult to swallow. "How was I to know that the horse was such a bloody goldmine. I thought he was a piebald they'd ripped off. But nothing valuable. Nothing..."

"What the hell are you talking about?" Murty interrupted. "What piebald? You sold all your horses."

"The horse I was hiding on Highfern Row. I bunked off the day before it was due for collection. I figured the Hackett pup could manage to dispose of it. How was I supposed to know it was White Heat? They didn't tell me, did they? Then Eddie goes and does his thing on the blind bridge. And who's to blame? I wasn't even there and they're blaming me!"

Ben's knees jerked and threatened to buckle under him. Murty held him upright. "We never had White Heat on Highfern Row! I would have recognised him immediately."

"Not if he'd been dyed, smart guy!" Murty jeered. "Yes, dyed, and a good job it was too, good enough to fool all except those in the know."

Remembering the speed of the horse on Clemartin's Stretch, Ben knew immediately that Murty was telling the truth. He realised that in some hidden part of his mind he had always known the identity of the horse and had allowed himself to be fooled by the piebald markings, the belly-blaze that gave an illusion of roundness and took away the sleek appearance of White Heat. The enormity of what he had done swept over him. White Heat, the famous racer whose kidnapping had sent shock-waves through the racing world, was currently in his possession, sheltering in the middle of a wilderness. He listened, feeling dizzy with shock, while Murty continued the story, as revealed to him by a terrified Main Man.

Dessie Horgan belonged to a gang of thieves, who were given regular contracts to carry out specific robberies by a small but powerful group called the Reid Syndicate. Robberies ranged from spirits, to cigarettes, clothes, computer hardware and software and, in this instance, a horse. Main Man was not part of the gang. But, for the right price, he allowed Highfern Row to be used as a dropping-off point when goods were being shifted from one destination to another. The gang had dyed the horse and planned to keep him in hiding until the immediate fuss over his kidnapping died down. Then he would be handed over to the Reid Syndicate, who were organising the shipping of the horse to a destination in the Middle East. As Craigy had suspected, White Heat would be sold abroad and re-enter the racing world with a new appearance, new forged papers and a new identity. All this had gone according to plan until word reached the gang that the police had received information that linked them to the robbery. In panic, Dessie moved White Heat to Main Man's stables for a week until it was time to ship him out of the country.

"Now we come to the funny part of the story," said Murty, his face moving closer to Ben. "Horgan and his pals, including poor Main Man, were in mourning for White Heat. After talking to you, Dessie believed that the horse had been killed inside the horse-box when the crash happened. And you, you little horse thief, never made any effort to tell them the truth."

Ben wriggled against the moneylender's grasp. "No...I didn't...no!"

"Shut up and listen," hissed Murty, on a fresh wave of saliva. "Everyone was so relieved that the animal had been buried without any attention being drawn to him that they never thought to check out his identity, and poor Eddie was in no condition to enlighten them. However, I was under the impression that it wasn't White Heat, but an old hack with a moth-eaten coat that had sprouted wings and gone to his eternal reward on the blind bridge. Riddle me that one, please?"

Ben's body trembled so much that he slid to the floor when Murty released him. He rocked back and forth, his head buried in his knees, gulping air into his lungs. Murty guffawed and pulled him to his feet once more. "Too strong for your lily-white stomach eh? Enough of your shilly-shallying! Just tell me where that animal is hidden?"

"I don't have him. He was removed from the stables soon after the accident."

"Little liar!" Murty grabbed Ben's hair, lifted his face and slapped it hard. "Let me spell out the facts so that there's no misunderstanding. I want White Heat...now...this instant...yesterday. If you don't want to end up in intensive care like your boss, you'd better start talking, now!" He raised his hand again, but it stayed in mid-air. The sound of a police siren was heard approaching River View Avenue.

"Tell me...tell me...tell me!" He was shaking Ben, his face red with fury. When the police siren grew louder, he backed off. "I'll be watching you, smart guy. You'd better get used to a shadow dancing on your footsteps. We'll find that horse. And if you say one word about this, you'll never know what hit you."

When Murty left the stable, Mrs Hackett glared at him. But like the rest of her family she was terrified by this midnight intrusion into her home.

"Nice talking to you, Ben. We'll have another little conversation soon again." The menace in Murty's voice left Ben in no doubt about his intentions.

The three men slipped quietly out the front door.

"Horses have brought nothing but trouble into this house," shrilled Mrs Hackett. "And we still have trouble even when there aren't any here. I don't understand this at all and you'd better take that shut-off look off your face, Ben Hackett, because I know you're up to something. Your poor father's half-dead from all this carry-on." She moaned when Jean pressed an ice-pack to the side of her face.

"Now, now, Breda, it wasn't all one-sided, you know. I got a few good blows in myself," boasted Mr Hackett. "Did you see his right cheek? That was a fist and a half I gave him."

Mrs Hackett was scornful. "Let's see how you view the world through that left eye of yours tomorrow, Joe Hackett. That's if you can open it. Here, give me that ice-pack, Jean. Your father has more need of it."

Fire Fighter's ring on the doorbell interrupted her tirade.

"Say nothing about this or we'll know all about it tomorrow," she warned, opening the door.

The policeman looked at the broken ornaments on the hall floor. "Looks like there was a party on in Hacketts' tonight. Would anyone like to tell me what happened?"

"It's all right, Guard," said Mrs Hackett. "Just some of the kids acting the maggot."

"That's not the message we got from Mrs Toner."

"That interfering busybody!" snapped Mrs Hackett. "If that one had as much sense in her head as she has time for interfering in the honest business of other people, she'd be the brain of the century."

She looked guilelessly at the guard. "You have children, Guard. You know what they're like, little brats, every one of them. Mine let loose the pigeons and that caused a rumpus. Some of the birds even got into the house. Isn't that right, brats? You're all going to feel the flat of my hand on your backsides for this."

Faced with the combined innocence of the Hackett family, the police eventually withdrew.

Ben could not stop shaking. He pulled the blankets over himself and remembered the evening he had found Jip on the wastelands. It now seemed such an untroubled time, a time of dreaming innocent dreams and trying to make them come true.

"It's important to have a dream," he whispered, and wondered how to cope with a nightmare. When he slept, he heard the thunder of hooves on Clemartin's Stretch and he was beneath them. They hammered against his head and crushed him. He awoke, sweating. Violence seemed to be everywhere, from the casual brutality of

Main Man to the cold violence of Murty Slomes. Ben thought about the night rider, his head bent over the handlebars, riding his bike like a violent weapon over the blind bridge. Then he thought about his friend, Danny Moone, and the hatred he claimed to feel towards his father. Violence so close to love that it trapped him in a limbo-land of bonfires and cider parties that would eventually destroy him.

Ben turned restlessly in his bed, knowing that it would only be a matter of time before Murty found the horse. "Someone help me. What am I going to do?" he whispered. Dawn slid on a silver line over the horizon and into his room. But still he could not sleep and the shrill sound of birdsong was the only answer to his question.

20
Ellen's Visit to River View

For two days, Murty's men waited in a car parked outside the horseshoe of houses, an excellent vantage point from which to watch the comings and goings of the Hackett family. The two men made no effort to hide themselves and watched every movement Ben made whenever he went outside. As soon as he passed the car, one man would get out and follow him. No matter how many detours he took, the footsteps would stay the same distance behind him.

Ben was frantic with worry over White Heat. Even though the grass in the old schoolhouse was suitable for grazing, he knew that the horse was used to the routine of regular feeding and exercise. He was haunted by thoughts of the horse stumbling and breaking his leg. Or, seeking escape, wandering blindly around until he fell, senseless from exhaustion. Images of Murty and his men descending on the hide-out and removing him flashed continually through his mind.

There was only one person who could help him— who knew how to care for a horse as well as he did. Or perhaps it was just that he needed to hear her voice again.

In desperation he ran around a corner into a small cul-de-sac called River View Terrace. He noticed the door of a phone kiosk hanging open. He darted inside, hoping that no one had vandalised the phone. When she was away in boarding school, he had sometimes found himself looking up her phone number as if that slim contact would bring her closer. He had scoffed at his stupidity and repeated the numbers in his mind. Once he had dialled the number but hung up immediately he heard an officious voice saying, "The Pender residence. Can I help you?"

On this occasion he recognised Ellen's voice and although it sounded flat, without emotion, he sighed with relief.

"Ellen, it's me, Ben Hackett."

She gasped. There was a short silence before she replied, a frightened whisper floating down the line. "Why are you ringing me?"

"I need help, Ellen. I'm in terrible trouble." He wondered if it was his imagination when her voice lifted.

"Why? What's up? How can I help you?"

"Do you remember the time...the day before...before Jip died." He swallowed and glanced from the kiosk. But the man following him had still not appeared. "We were going to meet and I was to show you Jip's hiding place. Do you remember?"

Again he heard her sharp intake of breath. "Yes, Ben. I remember."

"If I told you where it was, would you go there for me?"

"Will you be there?"

"No."

"Then why...why?"

"Listen!" He cut across her hesitation and gave her the directions. She was so silent on the other end of the line that he could not tell if she was still listening. "Don't ask me to explain things now but I've hidden a horse there."

"What are you talking about? What horse?" She sounded tense and confused.

A burly man with cropped hair and warts on his chin rounded the corner and ran towards him.

"Ellen! I'm in trouble. I'm being prevented from feeding him by a guy called Murty Slomes. He's vicious."

"I know. I've heard of him. But what..."

"That's all I can say! Ellen, please, will you go there and see if the horse is all right? Please!"

Ben slammed down the phone on her urgent questions. He ran from the kiosk. The man grabbed the swinging receiver and yanked the wire from it.

Ben had no idea whether Ellen would respond to his appeal. Another sleepless night passed and, in the small hours, when he looked from his bedroom window, he saw the dimmed lights of a stationary car outside. The following day seemed endless while he played more cat-and-mouse games with Murty's men. It was evening time when Cindy answered a ring on the front door. She came into the dining room and smirked at Ben.

"Hey Ben, that freeze-the-breeze from Fairview Heights is at the door. Aren't we honoured. Dare I invite her into our humble abode?" She mimicked a posh accent and giggled when she saw her brother's astonished expression.

"What are you doing leaving her at the door, for heaven's sake?" Mrs Hackett shouted from the kitchen. "Have we no hospitality in this house? Bring the child into the dining room, you silly dopes."

Ellen had lost weight. Dark shadows smudged the skin under her eyes. She had cut her hair. The heavy black hair that used to rest on her shoulders was a tightly cropped cap around her face, so short that spikes jutted from the crown. Her eyes looked enormous, her neck long and thin. Chunky loops of silver and copper decorated her ears, which were pierced in different places along the lobes. She looked embarrassed, her hand instinctively touching the bare nape of her neck, as the younger members of the Hackett family slouched in chairs or on the floor, ignoring her and watching television. Yet Ben knew that they were sizing her up, and would tease him without mercy as soon as she left. Ellen looked shyly around the crowded room and the silence settled like a stone around her. He offered her a chair and she sat down.

"I...I...hope I'm not calling at a bad time?" she stammered, politely.

"Not at all," said Cindy. Ellen's uncertainty acted as a trigger and a hubbub of showing-off noise started. Cindy began arguing with Jean over which television channel they should watch. Maria screamed for her bottle.

Steve switched his Walkman on again and retreated into his own world of heavy metal music, while Dave, his twin, outraged and disbelieving, accused Cindy of using his homing pigeons as postbirds to bring love letters to her boyfriend. She vehemently denied this accusation by trying to jump on his foot when he started reading out one of her letters.

"Hold the baby for me. I just want to heat up her

bottle." Mrs Hackett came into the room, ignored the rumpus and, mistaking Ellen with her cropped hairstyle for one of her twins, absent-mindedly handed plump, red-faced, howling Maria to her. Ellen placed the baby on the edge of her knees and looked helplessly at Ben. "I've never held a baby before."

"Really," said Cindy, scornfully. "Lucky you. I've never done anything else."

Within a few minutes, Ellen was crooning over Maria, who, delighted with such undivided attention, had relaxed so completely that a pool of moisture was spreading over her minder's pale-blue jeans. Ben wanted to hide under the carpet but did not think it would be thick enough to hide his mortification.

"Em, Mrs Hackett! I...I...think Maria's done something." Ellen was mesmerised by the heat seeping into her knees.

Mrs Hackett whisked up her daughter.

"Oh, you bold, bold baby. Say sorry to the nice girl or she won't ever nurse you again." She deftly fastened a nappy on the baby and smiled kindly at Ellen. "Ah sure, don't worry about it, love. It's a sign of luck when a baby pees on you."

"Oh Ma!" her family groaned. But Ellen, after one look at Ben's face, was laughing in the same spontaneous way she had laughed in Charney House when he thought she was a ghost.

"I need to talk to you, Ben. Is there somewhere private we can go?" she whispered when she eventually returned from the bathroom. The washed patch on her jeans was like a map and he looked away, red with embarrassment. He brought her into the parlour which was full of shining ornaments and lacy chair covers, a cold room that no one ever used unless a stranger called. When he turned on the electric fire, it only seemed to add to the chill in the atmosphere.

"Did you find the horse?" he asked.

She nodded. "He's OK. I went there yesterday and today. This morning I took him for a run on the Stretch. But I won't be able to go again. My father's arranged time off to come with us for a week's holidays. He just told me this evening. It's a surprise because he missed my birthday party." Her voice was flat. "Will you be able to manage without me?"

"Don't worry about it. I'll think of something," he lied, swallowing his disappointment. Anxiety deepened the lines on her forehead and around her eyes.

"That's the same horse you were riding when Main Man attacked you. What's going on?"

"The man who was injured on the blind bridge was collecting that horse." Ben found it difficult to look at her. "After Jip died I took the horse to the field and hid him from Murty Slomes. He seems to think that the horse is payment of a debt that Main Man owes him."

Ellen's features seemed to collapse inwards with shock. Tears moistened her eyes but she did not cry. She watched him, noticing his uneasiness, his fidgeting movements as he crumpled a lacy chair cover between his fingers. "You're not telling me everything, are you, Ben? There's something else going on. If you trusted me enough to find the horse, then trust me a little bit more." She was trembling as if his words had spun a nightmare before her eyes.

He struggled with his desire to share such a dangerous

secret then cautioned himself not to be a fool. "None of this would have happened if Jip was still alive. He'd be safe in the hidden field!"

"Shush Ben, please shush...!" She placed her fingers on his lips, unable to bear the sound of his voice, then reached towards him as she had done on Highfern Row. His hands touched the curve of her back and drew her close. They stood like that for a long time, afraid to move. He was aware of her face pressed against his shoulder, felt her lips soft against his neck. Then they were staring at each other, shyly smiling, and he held her tighter.

"Ellen!" He swallowed and blew out his breath. "Am I mad to be falling for you?"

Her fingers made the back of his neck tingle. "I don't know," she whispered. "But things have been awful lately and I keep thinking about you all the time and wondering..." He leaned towards her, interrupting her. When they kissed, she gave a low instinctive cry of pleasure, and he answered her, wondering if he would ever have the strength to let her go.

"Will you be all right when I'm gone? What will you do about the horse?" she asked before she left. The anxiety had returned to her face.

"Don't worry. I'm going to sort it out. It's all under control," he lied and placed his finger on her lip when she demanded to know his plans.

"She's a nice enough girl," said Mrs Hackett, when Ben returned to the dining room. "But none of your daft loving, do you hear me, now!"

"Are you mad!" replied her son. "I wouldn't dream of it."

That night his sleep was restless with heat-filled

images of Ellen and he groaned, turned so restlessly that
he woke. In the bathroom he stared into the mirror. His
lips looked full, almost bloated with sleepy pleasure. He
shook his head.

"Ma's right," he muttered, softly. "It's daft, daft
loving!"

21

A Training Stint with the Champs

The occupants of the black car watched and waited outside Ben's house. At hourly intervals, Mrs Hackett fumed and demanded to know what was going on. "You talk to him!" she ordered Craigy, leading the blacksmith into the kitchen. "Look at him. A closed zip for a mouth. He has me driven grey with the worry of it all." She angrily ran her fingers through her frizzy blonde hair and leaned forward so that Craigy could inspect it.

"I'll talk to him, Mam. But it might be better if you left us alone for a few minutes."

"With pleasure," said Mrs Hackett. "But you'll be the lucky man if you can get one bit of good out of him."

Craigy pulled a chair over to the table where Ben was sitting. "I know you don't want me here, Ben. But I've heard stories and I've seen those gorillas outside the house. They've got the stamp of Murty Slomes about them. He's investing a lot of time in you and I'm not leaving until you've told me what this is all about. So come on, out with everything."

Ben tried to resist the voice. "You wouldn't understand!"

"It's police trouble, isn't it?"

Ben nodded, miserably.

"And you're afraid that if you tell me I'll make you go to them."

"Something like that."

"Well you're wrong. What age are you now Ben? You're gone seventeen as far as I know. You're a man. You're the one who makes the decisions now. I'm not going to force you to do anything."

"Honest?"

"Try me."

Ben could no longer close his mind to the sweet relief of unloading his problems. "I'm in this mess because Jip was killed!" he burst out. "It's not my fault. None of this would have happened if only—!"

Craigy let him rant for a few minutes before holding up his hand, demanding silence. For the first time since he entered the kitchen, the blacksmith's sympathetic expression had grown stern. "Listen, lad, if you get the facts out of the way first—then you might be able to see whose fault it is. So start talking!"

It was easy once he began. Craigy listened intently, his weatherbeaten face displaying no emotion. But his lips clenched with worry when he heard White Heat's name. Every time Ben's voice faltered, he nodded his head slowly and murmured, "Take your time, lad. Take your time."

When Ben finished speaking, Craigy's composure was under severe strain. "Well—you've certainly landed yourselves in a right mess. Why didn't you go to the police in the beginning?" he asked.

"I don't know," Ben muttered. "All that stolen stuff

had been coming to Main Man's cottage for months and I'd kept my mouth shut so that Jip could stay on in Highfern Row. Then he died and...and nothing seemed to matter any more."

He found it impossible to explain the anger and the grief and the loss that had churned up his thoughts in those hours following Jip's death. "I kept thinking that as long as I had another horse I could pretend that Jip was still alive. But it was only a dream and even that was as dead as Jip within a day. I didn't want the horse. But I didn't know what to do with him and I just let each day go by and...and...I really thought some kind of miracle would happen..." His voice trailed away.

"Miracle!" snorted Craigy. "It's a miracle you haven't had your hands cut off by that gangster, Murty Slomes. You've been a right foolish lad, and make no mistake about it. He obviously intends smuggling the horse out of Ireland and he won't rest until he gets his hands on him."

"Tell me what to do, Craigy?"

"No," replied Craigy. "I told you already that this is real-life stuff. If you are able to make irresponsible decisions, then it's time you learned how to make responsible ones."

Ben shivered. "I know what you're saying. But I can't go to the police."

"Have I told you to go to the police?" demanded Craigy. "I'm leaving it entirely up to you. I can give you all the support you need but I can't give you an easy solution to a problem you created yourself. You're in this mess because you, no one but you, took a horse that you knew was stolen. Even if you did not actually know it was

White Heat, it made no difference. You hid him with the intention of keeping him for yourself. What happened on the bridge obviously affected your decision. But no one forced you to make it. One of the first words you ever learned to say was 'No!'" Craigy was staring intently at him. The silence between the two of them deepened. Ben was bitterly disappointed. He had expected help from Craigy, not a lecture.

"Get out of here Craigy. I've got to sort this out myself."

"You'll do the right thing, Ben." The blacksmith rose stiffly to his feet. "I believe in you." He bent down, speaking in a low voice. "We can hide our mistakes, lad. Turn them into lies and live that lie, forever if need be. But where can we hide the thoughts in there?" He tapped his forehead. "They're the dangerous things. The buried thoughts. They're the ones that can destroy us. They're the greatest enemy of all."

After Craigy left, Ben rested his arms on the table and buried his face in them. He sat like this for a long time, cocooned from the sounds of the house that clattered around him. Finally, it was Susie Moone's bossy voice exhorting the Charney Champs to train harder that drew him out of his reverie.

She started her team-training session at seven in the evening and he realised that he had been hearing her voice, and the heart-rending groans of the Champs, floating through the open window for a long time. But the sounds had not penetrated the confusion in his mind. When he straightened and looked at the kitchen clock he was surprised to discover that it was half-past eight. The endless, circling, thoughts had stopped. His brain was clear as if he had worked out a long and difficult puzzle and, finding the answer, wondered at its simplicity.

He had to talk to Fire Fighter. Only Fire Fighter had the force to protect White Heat from Murty Slomes. Then he would be free from the worry that had tormented him since he first led the horse past the rubbish tip and out along the narrow country road towards the hidden field. Craigy would call it a guilty conscience. But Ben knew it was more than that. He had a gift, given to very few, a gift of understanding, a rippling wire of communication between him and the animals that became part of his life. No wonder he had been unable to give White Heat a name. The name had been deeply buried in his mind all the time, along with the knowledge that he was abusing this gift. White Heat belonged to the world and Ben Hackett must set him free. He would visit the field for the last time and make his peace with the champion. Somehow, that seemed very important. Then he would return to Stonyford Police Station and tell Fire Fighter everything. But first he had to find a way past the black car outside his house.

"What's up, big brother?" Cindy came into the kitchen. "I've seen happier faces on a morgue slab." She was dressed in her colourful tracksuit and was taking a short break before ending the session with a thirty-minute jog on the wastelands. She turned on the kitchen tap and splashed cold water on her flushed face, then sat beside her brother, jabbing him with her elbow. "Has the posh girlfriend let you down?"

"Mind your own business," he muttered.

"I suppose it's to do with that creep, Slomes. What's he got on you?"

"I'm hiding something and he wants it. Just don't ask me any more about it, Cindy...please! I can sort everything out if I can just get to the wastelands without them noticing me. I've got to shake them off long enough to get past the rubbish dump."

She sat quietly for a moment, then began to chuckle. "Come on! I've got a brilliant idea."

They climbed the fence into Susie's back garden. All around Ben, the Charney Champs were doing bending and stretching exercises prior to their three-mile jog. Since the day of Jip's funeral and Craigy's expression of belief in their invincibility, Susie was taking her position as manager very seriously. Three times a week everyone had to report for training. The only cry-off excuse, she insisted, was sudden death. Cindy talked intently to her manager and the two girls grinned in Ben's direction.

Susie gave a thumbs-up sign and when she stood before Ben, her eyes were bright with mischief. "If you're coming training with us tonight, Ben Hackett, you'd better get changed fast."

"Huh?" he said.

In reply she threw a tracksuit at him. "Go on, get changed. You can jog on the wastelands with us. Dressed in that tracksuit, you'll be as safe as a needle in a haystack."

"I know why you're called Champs," he said, hugging her so tightly that she growled.

"This body is valuable property. Watch where you touch, punk!"

"Hi lads! Give my regards to Murty!" yelled Olive Bricken, when they jogged past the black car. The Champs formed a human shield around Ben. "Ask him if he gave his poor granny back her pension book yet."

Ben quivered and kept running. Two wads of cotton wool in the front of his track-top kept slipping. "I've got crooked boobs," he growled at Susie, who had insisted on adding this final indignity to his disguise. "If you're going to be a Charney Champ you've got to have boobs," she had stated, before they left her house. Her merriment was low-key compared to the gloating whistles and comments from the rest of the team when he had appeared. To the Charney Champs, this was a great adventure.

They knew that Murty Slomes was out to get Ben Hackett, and, as many of their parents had suffered, and were still suffering, at the hands of the moneylender, they were delighted to be drawn into any scheme that would make a fool of him.

On the wastelands, Susie was merciless. "Lift your knees, Ben Hackett. You're supposed to be involved in a training session, not running in the geriatric games."

He glowered, sweated, cursed and lifted his knees higher. The thick sweatband was like a vice across his forehead while the backs of his legs felt as if they had been mangled in a mincing machine. Still, all things considered, after training with the Charney Champs, he was lucky enough to be able to stand.

"This is where I drop out," Ben told them when they reached the towering rubbish tip. It was smoking, throwing out heat and a welcoming, hazy screen. "Thanks a heap, Champs. I couldn't have done it without you."

He sprinted along the country road and quickly ran through the leafy entrance. The tangled branches soon swallowed him from view. The Champs' team song, a faint sound, was carried on the wind. "We've won, we've won, we've won, we've won."

22

Confessions in the Hidden Field

Ben was breathless when he stumbled into the clearing. For a moment he could not see the horse and his heart plummeted. "White Heat! White Heat!" he called and gave the high-pitched greeting with which the horse had become familiar. Immediately there was an answering nicker from within the ruins of the cottage and the horse appeared in the doorway with his ears pricked, welcoming the familiar sound of his name. When Ben stroked his neck he saw the white hairs lying flat and almost invisible against the brown coat. It was an artful disguise that not only changed the colour of the horse but also his shape. But the edgings of the white sock on one leg were clumsy, as if someone had grown careless towards the end of a long and arduous job. These tell-tale signs were noticeable only because his eyes were primed to acknowledge the incredible fact that this was the famous racer, White Heat.

"I'm saying goodbye, White Heat." His tongue moved over strange sounds and the animal stood close beside him, his body motionless. Ellen had once asked him to explain his thread of communication with the horses.

But how could he explain it to her when he could not understand it himself?

He stood in the twilit shadows of the ivy-covered cottage walls and experienced the strange, empty feeling of letting everything go, his mind blank so that he could hear only the heartbeat of the horse. It drowned out all other sounds until it seemed as if the animal's spirit was inside him, filling him with warmth, his mind alive with the scents of a world he could not understand, but could share for a brief and mysterious time. They faced each other, a champion racer and a young man, their hearts beating together, heavy breaths mingling, energy flowing between them, filling them with the strength and the power of the wind as it swept across Clemartin's Stretch.

The horse pricked his ears at the unmistakable sound of footsteps and the swish of leaves being brushed aside. A girl appeared in the clearing, wearing jeans and a familiar sweatshirt. Ben stepped behind the doorway and watched Ellen Pender, who gripped a black plastic bag of horsefeed in her hands, her cheeks flushed with exertion. When White Heat moved towards her, he whinnied and tossed his head in delight. Ben felt like doing the same thing. She dragged the bag to the plastic bucket that was used as a trough and emptied the feed into it. White Heat began to nibble, his bottom lip moving delicately while he ate.

Ellen glanced up suddenly. When she saw Ben watching her from the doorway, her face flushed even deeper. For an instant neither of them spoke.

He did not know who moved first, but it took only a few strides before they had their arms around each other. He was tense with passion when their lips opened, moist touchings that made them tremble and hold each other closer. Then White Heat butted their shoulders and slowly, reluctantly, brought them back to earth again.

"I thought you were on holidays?"

"It's been cancelled again. The usual thing. Some business deal in Spain that's not working out as fast as my father expected." She had recovered her composure but, attuned to every nuance in her voice, he heard the current of anger under each word. "I was tied up during the day but as soon as I was free I took some feed from our stables and cycled over to see if the horse was all right. Anyway, what are you doing here? Have the heavies gone on strike?"

She laughed when he told her about the Charney Champs. "I didn't notice them when I was cycling through the wastelands. All I saw was that awful cider gang."

"Yeah! They like to party at night. A bit different to the swank affairs on Cypress Hill that your lot go to, I imagine."

"The end result is the same," she replied tartly. "They all end up pie-eyed."

"Stay for a while." He sat on the grass, resting his back against the wall of the cottage, reluctant to leave the shelter of the hidden field. She sat beside him and drew her knees towards her, hugging them and resting her chin on her arm.

"Are you disappointed about your holiday?" Ben asked.

"No. Why should I be?" In a flat, matter-of-fact voice she talked about her father, about the business commitments that called him away so often. But she understood the pressure he was under and when he returned from Spain he would explain his reasons to her, making her feel that she was such an important part of his busy world. She did not look at Ben while she spoke. Boarding school had been difficult. She had had to leave Dark Sprite, make new friends, wait for her parents to ring, try to hide her disappointment when the calls did not arrive. "Busy! How I hate that word." Then, as if repeating a well-learned lesson, she laughed apologetically and said, "But I'm a very privileged person and I do appreciate everything he does for me." When Ben put his arm around her, she turned towards him and buried her face in his shoulder.

Twilight was deepening, dark clouds gathering beyond the trees. She glanced at her watch. "Gosh! It's after ten. I'd better go. I told my mother I was visiting a friend." She looked at White Heat. "We have to do something about that horse. You can't keep him hidden forever. And I can't help feeling that there's more to that story than you're telling me."

"You're right. I might as well tell you the truth. All of Stonyford will know about it soon enough. Just before you arrived, I was preparing to go down to Fire Fighter to tell him that White Heat is hiding out in this field."

"White Heat!" She gasped with disbelief. "I don't believe you. There's absolutely no resemblance between him and that horse."

"They're one and the same, Ellen. I swear it's true. I just wish I could wake up and find that it's all a dream." He told her what had happened, trying to ignore the horror on her face. "So, what do you think of that for a story?" He stopped talking and held his hands, palms towards her in a helpless gesture.

Ellen was panicking, looking fearfully around the clearing as if she expected the police force of Stonyford to come storming from the bushes. She drew a deep breath. "But why go to the police? Couldn't you just set the horse free and make an anonymous call to tell them where he is?"

"I could. But what if Murty and his men find him first? White Heat has suffered enough. I'm heading for Stonyford Village to talk to Fire Fighter." He traced his fingers over her face. "You'd better go now, Ellen Pender. I'd no right to get you mixed up in this mess."

"But I *am* mixed up and I'm frightened that we won't meet again. My own life hasn't been too marvellous over the last few weeks either. You were the only good thing in it. It's weird how things work out. Us together..." her voice trembled.

He hugged her, trying to keep her fear outside the circle of his arms. "I don't know what's going to happen to me. All I know is that I want to see you again. I've never wanted anything so much."

He was shivering in the night wind, drawing warmth from her until she sighed deeply and moved away.

"I'll meet you here tomorrow and you can tell me everything that happens in the police station." They walked towards the passageway. He lifted a briar that trailed over her head but the swinging hoop of one of her earrings caught in the thorns.

"Ouch! That hurt." Ellen winced, put her hand to her ear.

"Stand still," Ben ordered. "I'll have it loose in a second."

Thorns pricked his fingers when he loosened the briar and it snapped free. It was dark yet she stood so close to him that her eyes looked luminous. Something else was gleaming. It shone like a star. It was a star, pure gold standing out against the chunky coppery shapes that hung from her ear.

"That's beautiful." He touched the earring. His finger throbbed where the thorn had torn the skin and a spot of blood smeared the lobe of her ear.

"Oh! That old thing." The words were spoken carelessly. "My father gave it to me for my birthday."

"Where's the other one?"

She shrugged. "I don't know. I lost it on the same night. Not that I care. Horrible old-fashioned things."

He felt as if his breath would freeze in his throat. "I know where it is," he said. "I found it."

"Where did you find it?" Her eyes widened with surprise.

"On the blind bridge. It's now at the bottom of Four-Mile River."

She drew away from him, covered her face. It told him everything he needed to know.

"It fell off your ear when the motorbike went over the blind bridge. It probably fell off just a few seconds before Jip died! You were the pillion passenger!" He was amazed that his voice was so steady, seeing, once again, the black banner of hair, blowing wild in the jeep headlights, hands to her ears when the bike swerved and then disappeared, leaving devastation behind it.

She nodded, looked up at him. "I didn't...I wasn't...Ben! Stop it. Stop staring at me like that! I can't bear it."

"Tell me...tell me...who was riding that motorbike? Tell me! Tell me!" He shook her, just as Murty Slomes had shaken him in Jip's one-time stable. And his voice echoed in the same bullying tones. He remembered the time in Sallin's Lane when she came towards him under the arch of spreading branches, riding Dark Sprite. The trapped and angry feelings that swept over him as they faced each other. He remembered his envy, and the attraction that, even then, was like a dull ache in the pit of his stomach. They seemed such childish emotions compared to this loneliness of knowing. Her eyelashes were dark against her cheeks, her eyes unable to look up from the trampled grass under her feet.

"That night...the night that Jip was killed..." Her voice faltered.

"What about it?"

"You sound so hard. You're judging me before you've even heard my story."

"There's nothing to judge. A man is on a life-support machine. And my horse is...is...he's dead and nothing will bring him back."

"Don't you think I haven't thought about that! Every single minute of the day, and even when I'm sleeping I'm dreaming about it all the time. Ben...please make this easier for me!"

"Tell me," he repeated and, listening to her voice, he was back, once again, on the twisted arch of the blind bridge that divided him from Ellen Pender just as cleanly as it divided River View from Cypress Hill.

23

Memories of a Party on Cypress Hill

Sometimes she cried during the telling of the story. At other times she spoke in the same matter-of-fact voice that she had used earlier when she spoke to Ben about her father.

On the morning of her birthday, he had left for work before she woke. A single rose lay on her dressing table beside a small jewellery box. Ellen opened it and looked at the gold earrings, shaped like stars, dainty, delicate and very classy. Pieces of jewellery that she would cherish when she was twenty-one years old. But not for a teenage girl who liked chunk and junk on her ears. She knew immediately that Ms Page, her father's personal assistant, had bought them for her.

Her birthday card read: "To my beautiful girl. Sixteen kisses from your loving father. Tonight I want you to save the first and last dance for me."

When the salads had been prepared and the steaks were marinating in some succulent mixture, Manic Madness, the disc jockey, arrived to set up his equipment in the marquee that had been erected at the back of Fairview Heights. Her mother shuddered delicately, staring in dismay at the flashing lights and the massive amplifiers that Manic Madness tested out for sound balance.

The sun was dipping behind a bank of peachy clouds when the guests arrived. A barbecue was served on the lawn. There was still no sign of her father by the time they finished eating. The young people, encouraged by the persuasive yells of Manic Madness, started dancing in a wide circle.

"What on earth do they remind you of?" Mr Forester the butler asked Norrie, the housekeeper.

"Wild monkeys let loose after a long imprisonment," replied Norrie. "As for the music...!"

"I heard that sound once before," replied Mr Forester, thoughtfully. "When I had the misfortune to come upon the chassis of a train being battered into pulp."

At any other time Ellen would have found that funny. But she was just returning from her father's office, where she had been summoned to take his call.

"I'm sorry Ellen!" he had finally cut across her protests, using the tone of voice that ended all discussions. "Don't go on so much about it. I've got a late meeting. It's an emergency. Ellen! I can hear the sulk in your voice. Be a good girl and remove it. Immediately!"

And because he sounded weary as well as impatient, she told him it did not matter that he had to work late on the night of her birthday party.

In the main reception room, her mother was entertaining the Barclaids. She glanced up when Ellen opened the door. "What is it, Ellen?" she asked, moving gracefully towards her daughter and lowering her voice.

"He can't make it. Even though he promised. I knew

he wouldn't make it. I just knew. It's like every other time!"

"Oh for goodness sake Ellen! Don't whine like that. Your father is a very—"

"Busy man!" She finished her mother's sentence.

"You sound quite impudent, Ellen. And please take that ugly, pouting look from your face. Your father left you a wonderful present this morning. Did you think of thanking him when you spoke to him?"

"No! But tomorrow I'll ring Ms Page and compliment her on her exquisite taste."

A crease appeared between her mother's trim eyebrows. It looked out of place, like a deeply embedded scar, and even when it disappeared, Ellen imagined its imprint marring the smoothness of her forehead. "Stop speaking like that! You don't know how lucky you are."

"Yes I do. You tell me so, a hundred million times a day. I don't want to be lucky. I just want my father occasionally to keep his promise."

"That's enough! You really are a most ungrateful girl. Go back to your friends this instant and behave like a proper hostess instead of an immature child. If you persist in this behaviour, I will ground you for two weeks and you will not be able to exercise Dark Sprite."

Her mother did not make idle threats so Ellen beat a hasty retreat.

"I will not cry! I will not cry!" she insisted. But it seemed wiser to go outside into the grounds so that no one could see her blotchy cheeks. It was impossible to make her mother understand that it was not just one incident that annoyed her. It was everything, all together, adding up to so many promises lightly made and just as lightly broken.

When Douglas Barclaid beckoned her deep into the shelter of the horse-chestnut trees behind the marquee, she ignored him. How long had he been standing watching her? She could imagine his sardonic grin. "Audrey told me to come and find you. She said you were sulking because David can't make the party." He always called adults by their first names.

"I'm not sulking!" Ellen replied, crossly. "I just want to be left alone."

Her parents refused to believe Ellen when she insisted that she could not stand one single rib, not one single cell of Douglas Barclaid's body. Two months ago he had tried to kiss her, pushing her roughly against the wall of the stables and jamming his knee between her legs. Afterwards she had washed her mouth out with a mouthwash that stung her throat. But still she could not get rid of the sticky feeling of his tongue pressing against her clenched teeth. Despite her objections, Mrs Pender had insisted he should receive an invitation to her party.

"Come on, cheer up," he ordered. "Let's get away from the kids' games for a while."

He grabbed her hand and because she had no desire to return to Manic Madness and his records, she ran with him until they reached the summer-house beside the lake. The trees blazed with fairy lights. The inside of the summer-house was a flickering glow of colours, merging together and settling over the two young people. Ellen noticed some bottles and glasses on the picnic table. She lifted one of the bottles. "Where did you get that vodka?"

"Where do you think?" Douglas smiled. "From David's supply. He won't miss a bottle or two. A few of us are going to party here, later."

"You had no right to touch my father's—!"

"Oh, come on, Ellen. Don't be such a pain. I'm your guest, remember." He challenged her with his eyes. "Go on, try it. It'll make you feel wonderful."

"I don't want to feel wonderful."

Douglas shrugged. "OK! OK! Don't take your foul humour out on me because your father couldn't be bothered coming to your party." Douglas was drinking from the bottle. His lips were moist, smiling at her.

She remembered the feel of his mouth and wanted to run far away from the strained atmosphere that he created in the summer-house. "That's not true!" she cried. "My father is a very busy man."

"My father is a very busy man," mimicked Douglas. "But something always comes up, doesn't it? There is always something that is more important than what his precious only daughter is doing." Douglas had a way with words. He used them like a whip, flicking them so that they stung and always landed on the most sensitive spot, right in the centre of her heart.

"That's not true!" She hissed at him. "You think you know everything but you know nothing! I hate you!"

She imagined he could read the angry thoughts in her mind and that he was laughing at her childishness. The liquid looked like water when he handed her the bottle. "Go on," he coaxed. "No one will know. You can't smell it on your breath. Take a few gulps and then you won't give a damn how many parties your old man misses."

She could smell something, faint and peppery. He was watching her, waiting smugly for her to refuse, to show her fear. If her father knew what she was doing he would be so disappointed in her. With a defiant toss of her head she raised the bottle to her lips. Her eyes stung, misting her vision when she swallowed. The fiery taste burned her throat and she shuddered, gasped. "It's poison!"

"Try it like this." He offered her a half-filled glass with white lemonade, smiling when she hesitated. "Go on. Give it a lash. Or are you still Daddy's sulky little girl?"

It was dark when they ran across the grounds of Fairview Heights, and Ellen was laughing as if they had just shared the funniest joke in the world. She had no idea why they were running. Or how many times Douglas had filled her glass. But everything was wonderful. The fairy lights spun in a kaleidoscope of colour. The night was humming against her ears and the ground was a see-saw, swaying beneath her feet.

The gate leading into Sallin's Lane was open. At the end of the lane they stopped, caught in the wonder-web of shimmering lights that lit Cypress Hill. They ran through the park where rows of saplings had been planted to form a shaded walkway. Douglas jumped and caught the branches of a sapling. The trunk was thin and fragile. It did not break easily but split into broken fibres, a jagged, moist tear that eventually snapped the slender trunk in two. He whooped, swinging from the branches of another tree. When he lifted her on to his shoulders, she grabbed the over-hanging branches, swinging wildly until silvery-green leaves showered over her hair. They left the maimed walkway and the saplings bent their broken trunks like a line of graceful swans dipping their heads under water.

When they reached his own house, Douglas made straight for the garage. The motorbike was well-oiled and started as soon as he turned the key.

"Come on, Ellen, get up." He patted the pillion seat. "Let's take this machine out for a run on the wastelands."

"Are you mad?" she giggled, fear beginning to penetrate the hazy glow surrounding her. "You can't take Ashley's bike out again."

He had put on a black leather jacket and helmet. "Who says I can't? He's still abroad. Come on! Don't be such a wimp."

She knew that he sometimes raced his brother's motorbike when his parents were out. She had gone with him once before, racing through the Stretch and then over the blind bridge, the wheels poised in mid-air on the summit for an exhilarating few seconds. She had trembled with fear and excitement as the wind whipped her long hair around her face. The wastelands had terrified her, especially when she saw the gang from River View gathered around the blazing bonfire. Afterwards she had vowed—never again, never ever would she take such a risk. Douglas was a speed-freak, and he loved an audience.

"I have no helmet," she yelled, but when he grinned, a challenge glinting in his eyes, and revved the engine, filling the garage with its urgency, she did not argue any further.

Afterwards, Ellen could vaguely remember speeding down Cypress Hill and taking the river road that led to Clemartin's Stretch, the blurred outline of cottages on her right, the murmuring flow of Four-Mile River on her left. The bike ate up the miles of Clemartin's Stretch until she screamed at Douglas that she must return to her party. She was beginning to feel ill, her head spinning from the noise and the speed and the alcohol.

"Let's do the wastelands first," he yelled back. She didn't want to go to the wastelands but his laughter drowned her voice and, even when she beat at his back with her fist, he ignored her. Her hair was a black banner, streaming behind her when they approached the sharp turn at the bridge that would bring them over Four-Mile River and on to the wastelands.

"The lights, Douglas," she screamed. "The traffic lights are red. Stop! Stop!" There was excitement in his laughter and her hands clutched the sides of her head, covering her ears to drown out the sound. Then everything around her was compressed into that one moment, the broad shape looming in front of the motorbike, the sounds and the smell of fear. There was someone running. Someone shouting, a call of desperation. Ben. But he was too late to stop the night exploding.

In that moment of horror, Douglas was moulded to the bike. His skilful steering managed to avoid the jeep and the horse. The bike swerved once more and then they were speeding safely towards the wastelands. But he did not circle the wild stretch of land. Instead he increased his speed, raced along the bank of the river until the houses were left behind and the river narrowed, winding its way towards the hill bridge that would bring them safely back to Sallin's Lane.

The party was still swinging. She knew that she was going to retch and retch and maybe, somehow, the night's events would be expelled along with the sour bile that was rising in her throat. When she was finally able to stagger to her feet, she entered the quietness of the stables and laid her head against the smooth belly of Dark Sprite. Of course, just giving her horse a name like

Dark Sprite did not make her into something magical. Yet Ellen felt some kind of magic. Maybe it was just comfort, or a warm energy that was wrapped up in sympathy, coming from the animal who breathed so evenly against her head. After a few minutes she patted her horse's nose and quietly closed the stable-door. In the clear lake water, she washed her face and made her way towards the marquee.

The following night she had cut her hair, hacking furiously, feeling that she was cutting through the last links with her childhood. It was so short that it automatically spiked across the crown, giving her face a stark, punkish look. Her father was furious when he discovered what she had done. So was her mother.

"So common, Ellen. So very common."

Ellen grimaced, remembering their consternation, her father's comment that she was no longer his "beautiful girl."

"If you only knew," she whispered. "If you only knew." Somehow his broken promises did not seem important any more. Like her long hair, they belonged to her childhood. She faced the fact that loving her father was not the same as liking him and that there were times when she did not like him very much at all. But that was nothing compared to the disgust and the shame that she felt towards herself. Somehow, this made it easier to lie to him and he was too busy to notice the tell-tale signs that he would have noticed in the past.

Now, standing in front of Ben Hackett, the wind was cold against the back of her head. For the first time since she had cut her hair, she missed the weight of it, the warmth of it around her neck. "Can you understand any of this Ben? Can you forgive me?"

She wept as she had wept so often since the night of the accident, walking alone along the winding roads of Cypress Hill, reliving the scene over and over again in her mind. "You don't know how awful I feel. I can't sleep at night. I keep thinking of that man on a life-support machine. And Jip. It's awful. The dreams! I wanted to tell you so many times. I can't cope with it, trying to keep it a secret."

He pushed her hands away when she tried to hold him. "Don't touch me! Stay away from me!" The skin on his face was a mask through which she would never again be able to reach him. "Why didn't you go to the police? You knew they were looking for information on that motorbike."

"I...I was frightened. Douglas wasn't supposed to ride that bike. He had no insurance or licence or anything. Can you imagine the trouble we'd be in?"

"I'm in deep trouble too. But that's not important. They expect the river rats to cause trouble. We're not privileged like your fancy friends on Cypress Hill." He mocked her, and she covered her ears, unable to listen to him any longer.

"You're no saint yourself, Ben Hackett. At least I'm not a horse thief!" She had stopped crying and was shouting at him, stamping her foot so hard that dead wood snapped and rooks flew from the trees, cawing angrily.

"So now we get to share each other's guilty secrets," he yelled back. "I hate you, Ellen Pender. Do you know what it's like to love something and have it taken away from you?"

Her anger left her as quickly as it had erupted. "Yes," she replied, very quietly. "I've just discovered what it's like." Then she turned, almost tripping over a hidden bough. Impatiently she pulled her leg free and ran from the clearing. The sound of snapping branches finally faded.

"She's gone," thought Ben, imagining her slim figure cycling towards the distant lights of Cypress Hill. Suddenly he began to tremble. His throat seemed to close over and turn into a hard lump and it was difficult to breathe. He wanted to hate her. Every part of him wanted to hate her until she was reduced to nothing more than a shadow over which he could walk. He wanted to fold her in his arms and kiss the sadness from her face. That was the strange awful thing, and he could not understand this anger and love that always seemed to exist together in his mind when he thought about Ellen Pender. On the blind bridge he had lost something special. But his loss suddenly seemed very light compared to the weight of grief she had to carry.

The horse was restless, his head and tail erect. Ben tensed when he uttered a snort, low-pitched, a danger signal. Ellen heard the sound when she emerged from the passage and bent to pick up her bike. She cycled faster, racing past the ferns and the hedgerows as if she expected to find devils lurking behind them. But it was too dark to see anything and the only lurking figures to watch her go were the two men who had been following her since the previous day when they had seen her leaving Ben Hackett's house. They smiled at each other when they heard the faint, guttural snort from deep within the bushes.

Diver took a mobile phone from his pocket and tapped out a number. In Stonyford Village the engine of a truck ignited and Murty Slomes, who had waited patiently for such a call, calmly slid the vehicle into first gear and headed towards the blind bridge.

24

The Final Confrontation on the Wastelands

A twig snapped. There was menace in the silence that followed. Someone was in the passageway. Ben could not hear a sound but every instinct told him that one, possibly two men were coming nearer. White Heat's ears began to flick. He was frightened, preparing to bolt as the tension closed around him. He snorted again, blowing air through his nose and lifting his head high. A rat scurried from the cottage. White Heat's hooves skittered.

"Steady, boy, steady." Ben encouraged the horse to stay calm. Leaves swished, branches broke, footsteps coming nearer.

"Get him!" a voice shouted. Suddenly there was a shape beside Ben. A man lunged from the passageway, hands pulling at him. Another movement, more hands grabbing for his feet; muffled curses when Ben kicked backwards, the heel of his boot making contact with a bent head; desperation lending him strength he never knew he possessed.

"He's split my skull." The man staggered away, clasping his head as if it were indeed going to split into two halves.

Before the two men realised what was happening,

White Heat lifted his forelegs and slashed his hooves in mid-air. The suddenness of his actions startled them, causing them instinctively to duck out of reach. Once more the horse plunged, lashing out with his back hooves before the men had time to move in again.

"That bloody horse is mad!" yelled one of the men. "I'm not hanging around here to have my head kicked in a second time."

Somehow Ben controlled the horse, his words loud and commanding. Quivering, panting heavily through his broad nostrils, White Heat eased out of his panic. Ben mounted him swiftly, bareback, and they began to move, towards the passageway. Branches whipped Ben's face and he bent his head, urging White Heat onwards. They emerged into the lane where Murty Slomes waited with his truck. The glare of headlights almost blinded the horse but Ben's voice never faltered, controlling, encouraging, calming White Heat, urging him into a sharp turn and away from the headlights. The horse's stride began to quicken. Murty roared at the two men to hurry up. When they emerged from the passageway, they had to leap aboard the slowly moving truck. Murty increased his speed but Ben knew that the truck would not pass him on the narrow lane for fear of injuring the horse.

There was no time for fear, just the sensation of his heart hammering in painful blows against his chest as White Heat began to gallop. Soon they were past the rubbish dump and on to the dark blur of the wastelands. This was a trial of speed and strength. The truck headlights swept across the wastelands, outlining the horse in its glare. Ben could see the glow of the bonfire. It was the only spark of reality in his nightmare.

The engine grew louder and there was no other sound in the world except the panting breath of White Heat and the roar of the truck.

They were approaching the blind bridge. Beyond it Stonyford Village would give Ben the protection he needed. But the truck was overtaking him. White Heat broke his gallop, staggered, terrified by the noise that drowned Ben's voice. He passed the turn for the blind bridge and bolted towards an unfamiliar part of the wastelands, where the grass was long, and rubble from the building of River View created dangerous humps in the ground.

"Steady, boy, hold it steady, boy," Ben tried to keep control. But it was too late. The truck circled the horse. White Heat stumbled and Ben went tumbling down, hitting the ground with a thud that made red stars explode inside his head.

A truck door slammed. Ben heard footsteps and tried to rise. But it was too late. Rough hands rolled him over. He tried to struggle, lashed out blindly with his fists. He called on White Heat to run...run...run.

Murty Slomes was above him, his face contorted with fury. His hands pinned Ben to the ground. "Tough luck, Hackett. You know too much. This'll make sure you don't talk about it."

There was pain, hot and sharp in his side, lifting his body so that it arched in a spasm. The earth began to spin around him.

"Oh shit! You didn't have to do that!"

Diver's shocked exclamation was swiftly silenced by the moneylender. "Cut the crap, will you? Do you want him running around Stonyford shooting his mouth off? Quick! Get the horse loaded. There's no time to waste."

Feet hesitated at his face, legs bent at the knees and Ben felt a hand on his body, a hand that trembled when it touched his side and pulled quickly away. "Murty! The kid's in a bad way. You shouldn't have…!"

"Shut your face and get into the truck! What the hell are you? A Sister of Mercy or something?"

White Heat tossed his head, terrified, his hooves clattering when they mounted the ramp of a truck. He gave a final loud snort before the ramp was slammed back into place and the engine revved, splattering dust on Ben's face when it passed him by.

Silence was a vast hole, full of memories. He could see faces hovering above him, familiar faces, but like the markings on White Heat, he knew they were only illusions. They flashed before his eyes when he whispered their names. He saw Sheba's bright eyes, winking at him. The dog, Brandy, running before him, a paint-tin lid clamped firmly between his teeth; Jip whinnying, "Follow me, follow me." Daft lovings that had once belonged to this life. Soon they too would disappear. He did not want to follow the shadowy images that were leading him far away from the wastelands.

He tried to lift his hand, to reach into the emptiness and touch his mother. But the pain in his side forced him back, breathless and sweating, into the long grass. He thought about her, heard her fretting, worrying about him, scolding him in her mind. The need to feel her hands on his face was an ache, buried in fear when he realised that he might never see her again.

There was another face that imprinted itself above all

the others, yet disappeared each time he tried to touch it. He would touch it, cling to it, call her name again and again, like a prayer. But the sound was trapped, lost and alone in the weeds and the heaped rubble of plasterboard and crumbling bricks. Ellen Pender was safely back in Fairview Heights.

The spinning sensation stopped. He was sliding down, deep down into a place where there was only pain. "I've been stabbed." His mind kept repeating the words in disbelief, unable to understand how his life could have been taken away so easily, so heedlessly. He released his breath in a slow wheeze. His hair, bleached from the summer sun, stuck to his forehead in wet tendrils. The wind was gusty, whirling around him, scattering the banks of tawny clouds that reflected the street lights of River View.

He began to shiver. The bonfire glowed for an instant before spluttering embers collapsed into grey ash. In the distance, the red tail-lights of a truck sparkled, drops of blood in the emptiness of the wastelands. Soon there was nothing left but the long grass, bending protectively over him as darkness slowly fell across his mind.

EPILOGUE

Danny

The night had begun badly and Danny Moone did not believe it was going to improve. Fire Fighter had warned them. No more cider parties on the wastelands. The gang had carefully chosen their spot, an isolated stretch of rough grass, shielded by a corrugated-iron hut that was used to store building materials. But when Billy Deane arrived with the news that Fire Fighter's squad-car was checking out the wastelands behind River View Slopes, they decided to call it a night and play cards in the van in Billy's driveway.

Danny refused to go with them. He wasn't afraid of Fire Fighter or of a night in the cells and anyone who tried to mind his business would soon know all about it. When the gang left he stretched his hands towards the flames. Then he lifted the flagon of cider to his lips and drank deeply. There were pictures in the flames and they eased the anger that festered inside him. Cider made the pictures brighter. It made him forgive his father, and when he was tired watching the flames they blurred and lulled him into a deep, peaceful sleep.

When he woke, the night wind had risen. He shivered,

his body stiff from sleeping on the hard ground. The cider flagon was empty. He tried to remember how much he had drunk. Above him the stars merged and swooped across the sky. There was a swooshing noise in his ears, as if foam-filled waves had burst through his eardrums. When he tried to talk, his words were slurred. Not that he could talk to anyone—even if he was able to do so. They had all gone home. And good riddance to them. He didn't need anyone.

Then he heard the thudding hooves. They seemed to shake the ground, and a loud cry rang out over the wastelands, a helpless cry, and for a moment he thought it was Ben Hackett's voice. They'd been friends once. Danny shrugged away the memory. That was a long time ago. Yet the memory persisted and he had a sudden image of Ben when he used to search for him on the wastelands. "Come on, Danny," he would plead. "Come on home now. Your ma's doing her nut…"

Danny raised his hands to his eyes, shielding them, and ducked instinctively as headlights almost blinded him. Something big was approaching, bumping over the rugged ground. Something that chased the horse and swayed when it passed the bonfire. The flames raged wildly for an instant in the gust of wind created by the speeding truck.

"Go home, punk!" yelled a voice. Or maybe it was— "Go home, drunk!" Was there a difference? Danny began to giggle. Then he heard it again, that same helpless cry, only this time it was far away and Danny Moone was drunk and it could have been the night wind blowing over the wastelands. He could not stop trembling. When he pressed his hands tightly over his ears the sound would not be silenced and kept echoing in his mind.

Someone else had heard it. Danny blinked and tried to stagger to his feet. It was that Pender girl from the hill, spiky hair and eyes glowing like some frightened night creature. She cycled past him without a glance. Her voice kept calling a name. Danny began to mimic her, slurred words repeating "Ben, Ben, Ben!" Then his mouth hung open on the word because she had seen the squad-car and was riding straight into its path, shouting in a high shrill voice about Murty Slomes and trucks that she had seen and hidden fields where dangerous secrets had been revealed.

The squad-car stopped and at a curt command from Fire Fighter she became silent. The policeman seemed to have lost all interest in the bonfire and did not even turn around when Danny taunted him. He spoke into the car radio and the girl from the hill curled herself into a ball and wept in the back seat of the car. The blue lights flashed on the roof. A spotlight fanned the darkness. A siren called out its warning. The car sped into the night. It was time to go home.

Danny staggered away from the bonfire. The strain of walking was great and sometimes he lurched from side to side. He fell once, stumbling into a hollow. Dried mud scraped his cheek.

His face rested in the long grass. Time passed or maybe it stood still. He tried to hide from the cars that were invading the wastelands, speeding in a path of blue light over the blind bridge and screaming like the wild Banshees in the stories his father used to tell him.

In the distance he could see the truck. It was returning

towards him, speeding, swerving, brakes squealing when the driver saw the police blockade stretched across his path. Danny heard the high whine of tyres sliding to a halt, Fire Fighter's voice shouting through a loudhailer, a horse snorting in terror and being calmed by Ellen Pender. Her voice was quiet now, and steady, as she led the trembling horse down the ramp at the back of the truck.

Danny rubbed his eyes and shivered. Those were images made from the moonlight and the shadows that haunted the wastelands. He had to get away or they would destroy him. At seventeen, Danny Moone knew very little about life. But one thing he did know was that turning his back on trouble and running fast was the only way of making sure that it did not catch up with him.

His father had taught him that one valuable lesson before he slapped his son aside and walked out of his family's life. In that last gesture he had taught Danny not to care. To care was to hurt. To lie awake at night and tremble with hope every time he heard footsteps mounting the stairs of Wheatfield Flats. To mark each day by the arrival of the postman. To return to the city, playing his mouth-organ, watching the people hurrying past, hoping, always hoping. A mug's game.

He stumbled deeper into the wastelands, towards a rugged place where the cider gang normally did not venture. But it was quiet there, away from the noise and the night-terror that he had felt all around him.

When he tripped over a heap of dusty plasterboard, his hand touched something soft. He pushed against it, trying to regain his balance. Slippery material crumpled beneath his fingers and it was wet, the cold, sticky feel of blood. He could smell it, sickly, sharp. A pale face was illuminated by the light of the moon. Danny's mouth watered suddenly and the cider spewed from him, stinging his throat, tears running from his eyes. He was not sober, yet, in that instant of discovery, his mind was crystal clear.

Ben Hackett was dead. He had to be. No one could lose so much blood and survive. It was not the first time that Danny Moone had seen a stab wound. But the pin-prick he had received from Main Man McMullen could not even begin to compare with the sight that he felt rather than saw beneath his fingers. He would be blamed for it. That was all he knew.

As he prepared to flee, he heard a moan. It wasn't a human sound, yet it came from Ben Hackett's throat, a thin kitten-cry. Danny hesitated. If he ran, he would never leave the flames of the bonfire.

Even when he was an old man, he would still see pictures in the embers. No amount of cider would dull the memory of that helpless sound.

He pulled off his sweatshirt and tied it clumsily around the wound. When he lifted Ben, he hung like a rag doll, a dead weight, and Danny staggered. The stars still meshed together and the ground rose and fell under his feet. But one foot followed the other as he moved across the wastelands. His mind was a void. One foot in front of the other.

He passed the bonfire. A piece of burned wood broke, scattering sparks that quickly died. There were no pictures in the flames. There would never be any more pictures. The young man in his arms made a sound, drawn from some strong and secret place within himself.

"Hold on, Ben!" muttered Danny Moone to his friend, putting one foot in front of the other as the lights of River View Avenue came into sight. "We're nearly home."

Also by June Considine
From Poolbeg

When the Luvenders Came to Merrick Town

Luvenders at the Old Mill

Island of Luvenders